GHOST DIVISION

D1295979

Also by Leo Kessler

THE IRON FIST
THE TRAITORS
WOLF
HELLFIRE

In the *Wotan/Panzer* Series:

SS PANZER BATTALION
DEATH'S HEAD
CLAWS OF STEEL
GUNS AT CASSINO
THE DEVIL'S SHIELD
HAMMER OF THE GODS
FORCED MARCH
BLOOD AND ICE
THE SAND PANTHERS
COUNTER-ATTACK

In the *Black Cossacks* Series:

THE BLACK COSSACKS
THE BLACK COSSACKS 2: SABRES OF THE REICH
THE BLACK COSSACKS 3: MOUNTAIN OF SKULLS

In the *Stormtroop* Series:

STORMTROOP
BLOOD MOUNTAIN

Leo Kessler

Ghost Division

Futura Publications Limited
A Futura Book

A Futura Book

First published in Great Britain by
Futura Publications Limited in 1978
Reprinted 1979

ISBN 0 7088 1447 6

Printed in Great Britain by
Hazell Watson & Viney Ltd
Aylesbury, Bucks

Futura Publications Limited
110 Warner Road
Camberwell, London SE5

GHOST DIVISION

BOOK ONE: THE FROGS

ONE: THE MEUSE, BELGIUM, MAY 13th, 1940

ONE

Blood ran down the gutters. A mess of gurgling red, frothing obscenely onto the gleaming pavement. The French dead lay everywhere in the shattered, burning houses which lined the west bank of the Meuse. Further up the street, panic had broken out. The Sengalese had thrown away their rifles and were running for the rear. '*Sauve qui peut!*' they cried, their yellow eyes wild with fright.

An officer of the colonial division, bare-headed, blood pouring down the side of his young face, tried to stop them. They swept him aside and he crumpled to the cobbles, his fingers scrabbling desperately for some support, muttering weakly. But the attackers were not having it all their own way. Bodies of some littered the far bank. Others floated face downwards in the water, while their rubber boats sank next to them. A wounded German hidden in the rushes screamed for a mother who would never come. Further back two Mark III tanks were burning fiercely, their flames turning night into day, the dying crewmen writhing in pools of brightly flickering fuel. The defence was costing the French heavily, but for the time being the armoured German colossus, which had crashed over the Belgian border so surprisingly only three days before, had been stopped. The Meuse Line held, and the river ran with blood.

Now, as the awesome red ball of the May sun started to slide over the hills behind him, the General braced himself against the turret of his Mark III command tank, its aerials whipping in the breeze, and focused his Zeiss binoculars. Behind him the firing had commenced. The whole weight of his divisional artillery was about to crash down on the ruins only a hundred metres away. But his practised eye told him the new barrage would do little good. The French gunners and snipers would only burrow deeper into the smoking ruins, to pop out again

11

once the bombardment had ceased. Then the slaughter of his unfortunate Thuringians would begin once more. The bad luck that had befallen the 7th Panzer Division in Poland seemed to have followed it to the Low Countries.

The General shivered slightly in his ankle-length leather coat, then swung his glasses along the length of the shattered waterfront, the rays of morning sun sparkling on the debris of war — battered cans of petrol, split ammunition boxes, tangles of barbed wire, abandoned guns, their wrecked barrels drooping like the snouts of dead, primeval monsters. How in heaven was he going to get the Division across?

Three weeks before he had proudly and confidently outlined to the *Führer* what his task in the coming campaign would be, and how he would do it. *Day One*: cross the Luxembourg frontier and drive into southern Belgium. *Day Two*: dash for the Meuse. *Day Three*: attack — crossing the river just below Dinant . . . Hitler had beamed at him and asked, half-bantering, half-serious, 'And, my dear General, what are you going to do then, eh?'

Without a moment's hesitation, he had replied. 'Unless I receive further orders to the contrary, *mein Führer*, I intend to drive to the West. You must then decide if my objective will be Amiens or Paris.'

There had been a gasp of disbelief from the other generals present at the final conference. General Busch, the commander of the 16th German Army, had sneered, 'My dear chap, I don't *even* think you'll be able to cross the damned river in the first place.'

Hitler had looked at him, the tension clearly visible on his sallow face. 'Well, General?' he had demanded.

He had given Hitler a flash of those steel blue, confident eyes of his, fingers briefly touching the blue-and-white metal of the *Pour le Merite* cross at his throat, Imperial Germany's highest decoration for bravery, as if reminding himself what a dashing young commander he had once been in the old war. '*Mein Führer*,' he had snapped, supremely sure of himself, 'on the

12

morning of the fourth day, the men of my division will be swarming out of their bridgehead on the *other* side of the Meuse.'

But that was now, the stocky little General frowned. That deadline had already been reached. His men were either burrowing even deeper into the mud on his side of the damned river or lay there, vacant eyes staring into eternity. The General made his decision. 'Operator,' he snapped at the black-uniformed radio operator, 'connect me with Colonel von Bismarck of the 7th Rifle Regiment.'

Moments later the aristocratic commander of his armoured infantry was on the radio phone. The General knew immediately that von Bismarck was shaken. There was something hectic about this normally imperturbable North German as he made his report. 'Heavy casualties, General . . . most dinghies sunk . . . fire from both flanks and front . . . commander of my motor-cycle battalion wounded, adjutant killed . . .'

The General listened as calmly as he could, then he barked, 'And what about tanks? Where's Rothenburg's 25th Panzer Regiment, in the devil's name?'

'I haven't had contact with him since midnight, General,' von Bismarck answered a little hopelessly. 'My last signal from Colonel Rothenburg was from Onhaye, five kilometres from Dinant—'

'Yes, I know,' the General interrupted impatiently. 'I don't need a lesson in the damned geography of Belgium! What gives with him?'

'The signal says he's bogged down there with thirty tanks in some sort of hollow.'

'Good.' The General forced himself to appear confident, although at that moment it seemed that all he had done was to get the first division he had ever commanded in one awful mess. 'Hang on the best you can. At ten hundred hours we'll attack again across the river.'

'Yes, sir.'

'Re-organize your men, get up there at the front yourself, and rally your regiment.'

'Yes, but General,' there was a note of despair in the

13

aristocrat's voice now. 'I need tanks – Mark IV swimmers to get my men across the river.'

'You will get them, Colonel,' the General snapped firmly. 'Now get on with the job.' He tossed the microphone back to the operator. 'Driver,' he barked, 'let's get out of this mess. Take me back to divisional headquarters.'

The driver needed no urging. With a roar and a shower of mud and pebbles, he swung the 20-ton monster round and set off for the East, leaving the death and destruction of the still unconquered Meuse gratefully behind him.

'Down!'

In the same instant that Major Kranz screamed his warning, the lone Beaufort dropped out of the morning sky, its twin Brownings spitting violet flame. Heinz, the blond gunner, obeyed immediately. Lead spattered the special Mark IV's turret like summer hailstones. Slugs howled off shrilly. Behind, the line of surprised tanks of the 404th Independent Amphibious Company opened up at the intruder as it barrelled down the stalled column, dragging its sinister, gigantic black shadow behind it, filling the morning with its unholy howl.

Major Kranz had time for neither the plane now, nor his command. A bullet had zipped inside the turret. It was screeching back and forth across the metal box. Ricocheting from side to side, unpredictably, behind, in front, and between the two petrified men, it missed them by a matter of millimetres. And then suddenly it had spent its energy. It slapped into the radio and died in a brief spurt of flame, at the very same moment that the lone raider zoomed off towards the crimson horizon.

'Phew!' Major Kranz sighed, his black Panzer uniform-jacket sticking to him with sudden sweat. 'That was a bloody close call, Heinz!'

The blond gunner wiped the back of his sleeve across his drenched brow. 'You can say that again, sir. It pressed the piss out of me all right.'

'Pressed the piss it did,' Kranz agreed, and with hands that

14

shook violently, he hauled himself out of the turret and looked back at his company.

The gunners were relaxing once again at their turret machine guns, the decks of the Mark IVs littered with smoking brass cartridge cases. No one had been hit, he saw, with a gasp of relief, though von Fromm's tank had taken a burst. All along the engine cowling there was a line of gleaming new silver scars. Kranz cupped his hands around his mouth and shouted above the barrage from the front, 'You all right, von Fromm?'

His second-in-command's cheerful young face appeared above the turret, the gold-rimmed monocle he affected firmly clasped in his right eye. 'Quite awright, sir,' he drawled with the lisp that he also affected in the tradition of his ancestors, who had served in the Prussian Guard since the days of Frederick the Great himself. 'Just a tiny bit wet-drawered.'

Kranz smiled wearily and turned to his front again. For the last hour his column of 'specials' had been stalled along the secondary road that led to the West and the Meuse. To his front the road was blocked completely by the terrified Belgian refugees who were now beginning to crawl out of the ditches on both sides. To the young Major's eyes, it seemed as if every garage, shed, barn and stable in the whole of Eastern Belgium had opened their doors to disgorge the mass of vehicles which barred any futher progress. Brand-new automobiles were mixed up with dog-carts and ancient farm carts drawn by equally ancient farmhorses. All of them were filled with frightened grannies and screaming children, with, here and there, sullen younger men, both bitter and ashamed of their own betrayal of their country's cause.

'Well, bit of a bawsup, isn't it, sir?'

Kranz looked down. It was Captain von Fromm, his long blond hair now neatly combed and sleeked back almost to the nape of his neck once more. He nodded morosely and watched as a couple of men in cloth caps and sabots started to re-tie a mattress on the roof of an ancient steaming Peugeot once more, as if it would keep out any raider's bullets.

'What do we do, sir?'

Kranz shrugged. 'If I were a dashin' young von Fromm,' he answered slowly, 'I'd crash into them and roll the poor bastards out of the way. Nothing must stop the Guard, what?' He raised his voice as he echoed the young aristocrat's favourite phrase.

Von Fromm smiled up at him, his eyes wrinkled against the blood-red glare of the sun.

'But I'm not a von Fromm. I'm just a reserve officer, who has been given this meteoric command,' he gestured at the fifteen tanks with mock pride, 'because of my technical knowledge rather than my military panache.'

'So no rolling our tanks over the civvies?'

'No. The civilians stay where they are. Besides, von Fromm, what's the hurry? We've got all the time in the world to find Army HQ. The 404th is being saved for a special mission.' He smiled a little wearily. 'I doubt if we'll see any action until the Invasion of England.'

'I reawwy think I should have joined the inf——'

But Captain von Fromm never finished his sentence. At that moment, there was a sudden howl of sirens to their front. Hurriedly the civilians started to scatter on both sides. Children screamed with fear. Old men yelled in protest. Younger ones shook their fists. But nothing seemed to stop the approach of the lone Mark IV. Its myriad aerials whipping back and forth, it shoved the pathetic junk the refugees had brought with them out of the way, rolling over their treasures, ripping up dolls, kitchen pots, clothes wrapped in bedsheets, with its brutal metal tracks. The General standing rigidly upright in the turret stared straight ahead at some distant object known only to himself.

'God awmighty!' von Fromm whispered hurriedly. 'Are my eyes faiwing me? A general up this far front!'

Hurriedly Kranz adjusted his black peaked cap with its death's head emblem as the strange Mark IV rattled to a halt facing his own tank, its sirens dying with one last wail.

For what seemed an age, the General stared at him with his unwinking blue eyes, and Kranz had the impression of a

16

ruthless, burning energy which would be stopped by nobody or nothing.

'Your name and unit?' the stocky little General barked and Kranz noted the trace of a Swabian accent. Now he knew where the toughness came from: the Swabians were renowned for it.

'Major Kranz, 404th Independent Amphibious Company, fifteen Mark IVs, four officers, sixteen NCOs, sixty other ranks, *General*!'

'Thank you, Major,' the General touched his hand to his peaked cap casually. 'Did you say, *amphibious*?' he asked.

'Yessir.'

Behind them, the refugees had begun to load their treasures once again, little realizing that at this moment something was happening on this remote Belgian country road that would catapult this stocky General into legend for both friend and foe.

'And what are your orders, Major?' the General asked, a sudden note of caution in his voice.

'To report to General von Kluge's headquarters, sir, and place ourselves at the disposal of Army Group!' Kranz snapped.

'I see.' The General hesitated for an instant only. 'Well, those orders are cancelled forthwith.'

'*What*, sir?'

The General gave him a wolfish grin, two deep lines appearing at both sides of his broad, determined mouth. 'I think you heard me correctly, Major. But I shall repeat my words. Your orders are cancelled. Instead you will report to the HQ of the 7th Rifle Regiment commanded by Colonel von Bismarck. Never fear, I shall take care of the Army Group thing. Hans von Kluge knows me well. He'll understand.' Again he grinned. 'He'll have no choice.'

'I see, sir,' Kranz answered in a faint voice, overcome at this sudden change in his fortune. 'And to what division does Colonel von Bismarck belong, sir?'

'The 7th Panzer. But seeing that you are now joining us, Major, you may call it what the rest of the Army does.' The grin vanished now to be replaced by a look of grim determination. 'They call it the Ghost Division, because it moves and strikes like lightning and is not actually seen until the fighting is over. Speed, Major, and cunning. The elements of surprise – and victory!' The General bent and snapped something at his crew below.

The driver gunned his engine, as if impatient to start.

Kranz raised his voice. 'Sir, just two questions.'

'Hurry it up, Major, the situation is critical. I have a lot to do this morning.'

'Where will I find Colonel von Bismarck?'

The General thrust a thumb over his shoulder. 'At the front, of course. That is where you will always find the Ghost Division as long as I command it. Now your other one.'

'Your name, sir? I must know who gave me my new orders so—'

'Mark it well,' the General cut his explanation short. 'The name is Rommel. General Erwin Johannes Eugen Rommel . . .'

TWO

In single file the Mark IVs waddled along the bank, rumbling through the mud and reeds, 75mms trained on the steep opposite bank. Crouched at the water's edge, dinghies ready to push out, the battered infantry of the German 7th Rifle Regiment waited for the signal. Up above, Colonel von Bismarck tensed. So far, so good. The French had not opened fire. Had they fled after their near defeat of the night? Or, regarding their defence of the Meuse crossing as a victory, were they waiting in the smoking houses to open fire once again as soon as the dinghies pushed off? Colonel von Bismarck did not know.

Rommel had promised him the Knight's Cross if he got across successfully this time. But the Swabian General had also warned him he would be fired if he failed a second time. He had no choice. His poor infantry would have to pay the price of finding out. He raised his Very pistol and pulled the trigger.

A faint hush and the signal flare exploded above his head in a burst of crimson. The Thuringians did not hesitate. They started pushing out their frail rubber boats at once, while the swimmers waded into the water at their sides, preferring to take their chance that way. The second assault crossing of the River Meuse had begun.

'Now take it nice and easy, Kurt,' Kranz said softly over the intercom, knowing that he must not make the driver hidden below his feet nervous. The terrain was very tricky on the river bank. One mistake and the tank could sink into the deep mud of the river's edge, and then it would be a sitting duck for whatever enemy guns were sited only half a hundred metres away.

'Easy it is, sir,' Kurt's young voice answered, as he edged the Mark IV along the track between the cliff and the mud bank, his engine overheating and roaring away crazily in the lowest gear.

19

Kranz turned to Heinz, the gunner. 'Swing round the turret and draw a bead on them. I'll take care of the smoke dischargers myself.'

'Yessir,' Heinz answered, his face gleaming with sweat in the green light of the buttoned-down hatch. He pressed the switch and the eight-ton turret started to swing round noiselessly. Behind them tank after tank did the same. Now fifteen 75mm cannon were directed on the opposite bank, like the guns of some wooden man-o-war about to fire a broadside.

Kranz licked suddenly dry lips, his fingers curling round the trigger of the smoke dischargers. If the French still occupied the opposite bank, they would open up any moment now. Below, Kurt touched his foot lightly to the accelerator. The Mark IV lurched forward, crashed through a tangle of brambles, pivoted alarmingly for an instant, as if it might overturn and slip into the mud, before rolling down smoothly with a loud splash into the River Meuse.

With an obscene, stomach-churning belch, the mortar opened up. Once, twice, three times. For one frightening instant, the infantry half-way across the river could see the deadly black bombs hurtling up into the blood-red sky, then they had vanished. But not for long. In huge fountains of boiling white foam they exploded in the river, rocking the frail rubber boats filled with ashen-faced frightened infantry.

The next salvo landed right on target. Dinghies disappeared in bursts of furious spray. Headless, limbless men hurtled through the air, before slapping lifelessly into the bank. The swimmers dropped their weapons. Screaming and spluttering with panic, they struck out for the shore, fighting their way through the wreckage and the dead.

The first of the attacking infantry began to stagger up the bank at the other side. Machine guns opened up. The Sengalese, their broad black faces wild with gleaming excitement, swung their guns back and forth, slaughtering the men in field-grey. Bodies piled up on the mud below. Men were wounded, and wounded again. A sergeant-major tried to lead an attack up the

20

mud-bank. He was cut in half before he had gone five metres, his upper body left clinging to the bank, his legs slithering down out of control. The men who had followed him dropped down again, cowering there at the water's edge, heads buried in their hands, sobbing hysterically like frightened children.

Now the French 75mms had commenced firing. The short-barrelled World War One cannon were ideal for this job. They lobbed shell after shell into the men still half-way across the Meuse.

'My God, oh my God,' Colonel von Bismarck sobbed, '*my regiment!*' Behind him, his adjutant screamed at the artillery liaison officer, 'Well, don't stand there, man! Get some smoke ordered down. *Smoke, for Chrissake!*'

The survivors started to clamber back to the east bank, eyes wide and staring with shock and fear. Boats filled with dead and dying, lying in their own blood and gore, drifted helplessly down the river. A rifleman, hand clasped to a gaping shrapnel wound in his shoulder, staggered by von Bismarck. 'Didn't have a chance, sir,' he gasped. 'Not a chance . . .'

A young officer, helmet gone, uniform soaked, hands and knees smeared with grey mud, tried to report to the ashen-faced Colonel, but no words would come. He was too shocked. Another man crawled by, dragging his leg behind him, not realizing that he was tearing apart the remaining skin that still attached it to his thigh.

Colonel von Bismarck looked at his adjutant, aghast. 'It's a massacre, Hans . . . a massacre . . .'

'FIRE!'

The fifteen 75mms crashed out a tremendous broadside in the same moment that Kranz, followed by the rest of the tank commanders, fired his smoke dischargers. The smoke flares spurted twenty metres above the water and exploded. In a flash there was thick white swirling mist to the 404th's front. It had gone exactly as Kranz had planned. 'Spread out . . . spread out, now!' he commanded over the intercom. '*Now!*'

Trained together at Berlin's Wannsee Lake, the commanders

did as ordered, spreading out immediately, putting a distance of at least twenty metres between each tank in anticipation of the enemy barrage which might well fall upon the smoke cloud at any moment.

Now the Mark IVs were up to their turrets in wildly swirling water, the snap and crackle of the river battle deadened by the sudden fog. Kranz risked popping his head up above the turret. He could see nothing save the white mist, but the little spurts of water to both sides indicated that the enemy were reacting. They were trying to range in on the tanks. He pressed the throat mike. 'Speed her up, Kurt.'

'Doing my best, sir,' Kurt gasped.

'I want better, unless you'd like a dirty big Frog shell to come down there and shake you up.'

'Nothing must stop the Guard!' von Fromm's affected tones crackled cheerfully over the ether. 'What?'

'We're not yet there, von Fromm,' Kranz snapped harshly. 'Now get the hell off the air!'

The tanks swam on. Now the fog was beginning to clear and the first French shells had started to plummet down among them, rocking their 20 tons easily with the impact, as if they were ships at sea struck by a sudden tempest.

Now Major Kranz, his throat suddenly parched, could see the opposite bank and the dark figures of French soldiers scurrying from the cover of a wrecked house to set up a machine gun, obviously intended to bar their progress. Instinctively he pressed the trigger of the turret m.g. It chattered into violent action. The running Frenchmen were bowled over instantly, throwing up their hands in crazy abandonment as they were hit, noiseless screams coming from their gaping mouths.

The water became more shallow. They had almost reached the bank. Kranz ignored the shell fire. As the Mark IV hit the mud bank, he willed the driver to make it, knowing that below Kurt would be lathered with sweat. It was going to be a tricky ascent.

Kurt bit his bottom lip with concentration. He knew if he gave it too much power, the tracks would begin to slip on the muddy surface of the ascent. If he gave it too little, the engines would stall and the Mark IV would slip down back into the water. With all his strength and experience, his ears straining to catch the slightest change in the sound of the motor, he fought the 20-ton monster up the incline, the sweat collecting in great opaque pearls on his eyebrows and dripping down onto his nose.

Behind them one of the Mark IVs received a direct hit. It went down to the bottom of the Meuse like a stone, sending up great obscene belches of trapped air. Neither Kurt nor Major Kranz seemed to notice. All their attention was concentrated on getting up the damned bank.

They were three-quarters of the way up. Suddenly, the left track encountered a clump of brambles. But instead of pressing them down with its weight, the Mark IV began to climb them at an impossible angle. Kranz caught hold of the turret just in time, his heart beating like a trip hammer. There must be a boulder or some sort of obstacle concealed beneath the bushes. He gasped. The Mark IV was trembling violently, as if it had a life of its own. *It was going to keel over!*

He opened his mouth to shout a warning to the crew to bale out. Next to him, Heinz, the pious Bavarian Catholic — at least on Sundays and religious holidays — crossed himself hurriedly, his lips muttering a fervent prayer. If they keeled over now, they were as good as dead. The French would not give the trapped crew a chance, Kranz knew that. In one more moment he would shout.

Suddenly the left track crunched down on the earth, breaking through the brambles. The trembling ceased. Below, Kurt breathed out a great sigh of relief and pressed his foot down on the accelerator. The track gripped immediately. A few seconds later they had cleared the top of the bank in a shower of mud and were racing forward to the sound of the battle, savagely chewing up the bodies of the dead French gun crew, the tracks abruptly red with their blood.

Paralysis descended upon the French positions as the massed

23

guns of the Boche tanks that had sneaked across their flank opened up. In their rifle pits and ruined cellars the *poilus* − men and officers − huddled to the stinking corpses of their comrades in fearful anticipation, bodies tucked into tense balls.

With a great roar, the barrage straddled their waterfront position. Shells burst with deafening thunder. All hell was let loose. Purple searing flame scorched their limbs. The choking stink of cordite filled their nostrils. The blast grabbed the breath out of their lungs. Shrapnel as big as a man's fist hissed through the air, cutting down everything in front of it. Screaming, sobbing soldiers fell on all sides.

A loud echoing silence followed, broken only by the cries of the dying. Again the *poilus* tensed. They knew the Boche, hidden from sight beyond the rise, would fire again. They did. The guns erupted into violent life once more. Fourteen shells winged their way towards the French positions. Faces ashen with shock, eyes wide, wild, and threatening to burst out of their sockets, the soldiers moaned as their pits and holes shook and swayed with the effect of that tremendous bombardment at such close range. Here and there those officers who could still think straight eased their pistols out of their holsters. They knew what must soon come.

It did.

Again the Sengalese broke. Throwing away their rifles, screaming with fear, skidding and sliding in the mud and gore, fighting each other in their panic-stricken haste, they started to stream to the rear. Enraged officers tried to bar their progress or fired madly at their fleeing backs. To no avail. There was no stopping the terrified Africans.

There was worse to come.

Now the black NCOs of the 14th Colonial Regiment started to give up. 'Hitler no come to Senegal!' they cried in broken French at their angry officers. *'We go home!'*

In vain the officers tried to stop them. They, too, started to throw down their weapons and leave their positions.

Behind the ridge, the German tanks changed over to high-explosive. Shrapnel flew everywhere. A coloured corporal went

24

down, his whole back slashed open, thick red gore oozing over the coal-black. But as he died, he still cried, 'Hitler no come to Senegal . . . *We go home!*'

Now the NCOs were also running. In his command post, the grey-haired Colonel with the medal ribbons of the First World War ablaze on his chest, pulled out his pistol, said a quick prayer for forgiveness, and shot himself. Frantically, his second-in-command reached over the dying body and whirled the handle of the field telephone desperately. 'For God's sake,' he cried, 'send tanks. The Boche are coming. *Send tanks . . .*'

'Driver – *advance!*' Kranz cried.

All along the ridge, the commanders gave the same order. The 404th was going into their first battle. At 40 kilometres an hour, they rattled across the flat bank towards the village, ignoring the tracer which bounced off their half-metre thick armour like golf-balls.

'Reawy, this is what I've been waiting for,' von Fromm's affected voice sang out cheerfully from the radio. 'Battle at last!'

'Keep your eyes peeled for Frog tanks,' Kranz said sourly. He could never understand people like von Fromm who seemed to love this murderous business as if their whole previous life had simply been a preparation for it. He nudged the gunner. 'Slip in an AP,[1]' he ordered. 'You just never know.'

'Sir!' Heinz answered. Smartly he ejected the gleaming high explosive shell from the 75's breech and thrust home the shell they would need if they met enemy armour.

Kranz occupied himself with the periscope, keeping his head well below the cover of the turret, just in case there were Frog snipers about, eager to add another notch to the butt of their rifles – in the shape of a German tank commander. The French were definitely abandoning the village. He could see their black soldiers running helmetless and weaponless up the cobbled street heading for the woods beyond. Victory was in sight. He'd roll through the village, consolidate and then radio his new division to send over infantry to hold it.

[1] Armour-piercing shell.

'*Sir!*' Heinz's excited voice cut into his plans.

'What?'

Heinz, crouched over the periscope at the opposite end of the turret, shouted, 'Frog tanks. S-35s, I think!'

'Where?'

'At ten o'clock!'

Feverishly Kranz swung his periscope round. Three squat shapes slid into the oblong of gleaming calibrated glass. 'Christ on a crutch!' he muttered. They were S-35s all right, and they were heavier and quicker than the Mark IV. The only advantage that the Mark IV possessed was its heavier gun – a 75mm to the enemy's 47mm.

He pressed the button on the radio mike. 'Von Fromm, take troops two and three and clear the village. Contact von Bismarck at once when you've done that and tell him to send over infantry. I'll take troop one and tackle the Frogs.'

'But sir—'

'Do as ordered,' Kranz cut him short. He was not going to risk any more lives the way the dashing Prussian aristocrat would. He would tackle the S-35s in his own way. 'Troop one,' he ordered, 'follow me!'

In a wide V, with Kranz's tank at the point, the four Mark IVs rolled forward on a collision course with the French.

The commander of the enemy tanks reacted immediately. His orders had been to support the colonial infantry. Now he prepared for a tank battle. Using the advantage of his superior speed, he spurted with his tanks to the cover of the nearest hillock and went into a hull-down position.

Kranz cursed. The Frog must be an experienced tank fighter. With his hull buried in the earth, only his cannon visible, it was almost impossible to knock him out. As the first enemy tank opened up with its 47mm, he cried over the intercom, 'Spread out, Max and Willie! Try to outflank them. The others, stay with me. We'll draw their fire.'

He could hardly wait for the two tanks to report they understood before he rapped: 'Kurt into that ditch. Helmut, do the same!'

Kurt needed no urging. At top speed, he rammed the Mark IV's glacis plate deep into the ditch which had loomed up in front of them. A moment later the other tank joined him.

The French commander saw the danger to his flanks. As one, the three S-35s opened up on Willie's tank. Kranz watched horrified through the periscope as the armour-piercing shells, trailing white tracer after them, hurtled towards an unsuspecting Mark IV. All three found their mark. The tank did not have a chance. Its eight-ton turret flew high into the air, as if it were made of paper. In an instant it was a mass of blazing blue flame, with the tank commander lying burning, sprawled half-way out of the turret.

The Frog had won the first round. Now his gunners were swivelling round their turrets to tackle the danger from the other flank.

'In the devil's name, Heinz, don't stand there like a spare dildo in a convent!' Kranz bellowed, his face purple with rage. 'Fire!'

'But it's no good, sir. I can't hit him in that position!'

'Blind the bastards at least. We must take the pressure off, while he's still got a chance.' Desperately he grabbed the turret machine gun and fired a wild stream of red, angry tracer at the dug-in enemy tanks.

The Mark IV shuddered slightly. Its first shell hurtled towards the S-35s. Automatically Kranz pressed the extractor-fan button, his gaze following the path of the shell. As he had anticipated, it landed harmlessly in front of the hull-down enemy tanks.

'Damn!' Heinz cursed at his side.

'Fire again,' Kranz ordered.

'What about HE sir?'

'Of course, it might blind them!' Kranz answered, grateful for the suggestion, clutching at straws, knowing he was making a hell of a mess of his first tank action.

Swiftly Heinz rammed home a high explosive shell. Two hundred and fifty metres away, the enemy tanks shuddered as their 47mms opened up. Earth and pebbles fountained into the air. The Mark IV, scurrying for cover, shuddered violently and for an instant disappeared into the brown flying mass. Kranz prayed. *Let him make it!* The cloud of earth disappeared – and the tank was still there.

Now Heinz fired. The HE shell exploded directly to the side of the French tanks. Smoke and earth blinded the French gunners. It was the opportunity Max had been waiting for. Engines going all out, the tank's driver crashed into the first of the firs. The thin trees snapped like matchwood. He slashed through half a dozen gears to stop the Mark IV from stalling. The engines didn't fail him. Next instant the tank was buried deep in the wood, out of reach of the French fire and to the Frenchman's rear. Now Kranz knew he could start attempting to knock the enemy out.

The shell slashed through the air. Metal splinters pattered against the tank's glacis plate. Kranz ducked instinctively and fought back his fear as the tank pushed back on its rear sprocket under the impact like a frightened horse.

'Mary, Joseph, Jesus!' Heinz gasped. 'That Frog is closing in on us.'

Kranz did not answer. He could not. Instead, he fumbled with his radio mike, desperately licking his parched lips. 'Max,' he finally managed to croak, 'do you read me?'

'I read you, sir.' The tank commander's voice crackled metallically in his ears. 'What now, sir?'

'What's it look like at your end?' Kranz asked.

'Two have turned to face the wood, one is still pointing its gun in your direction, sir,' the tank commander said.

'*Bitch!*' Kranz cursed. They were to the back and front of the hull-down French tanks, but all the same they could not move into the open without risking being knocked out. What was he to do? Another mass of metal burst and shook his tank violently, sucking the very air out of his lungs. Suddenly Kranz was overcome by a strange euphoria, a compound of fear and anger. He did not know it then, but before his short life ended in a nameless Russian village, he would experience the sensation many times. It was the blood-rage that possessed young men and made them forget all else in one overwhelming desire to kill.

'Driver!' he cried. '*Advance and meet the enemy!*'

28

THREE

'*Sale con!*' *Commandant* Bastian cursed, half fearful, half amazed. 'What in heaven's name is the Boche up to?' He peered at the lone German tank which was rattling towards him, making no attempt to use the terrain to cover its approach, wide open to the concentrated fire of his and the other S-35s' cannon.

'Suicide, *mon commandant*,' Jo-Jo, his big Niçois gunner chuckled happily, raising his brawny, tattooed arms to thrust home an armour-piercing shell. 'The Boche is afflicted by their well-known death wish – Jo-Jo Gabriel is the man to fulfil that wish for them.'

Commandant Bastian laughed, isolated in his commander's turret, away from the rest of the crew, unlike the German practice. 'Be my guest, you big blowhard,' he cried over the intercom. 'Let me see if you can shoot as well as you can boast.'

'I'll slot it in him, as easy as swatting a dead fly on a wall,' Jo-Jo said confidently and pressed his right eye to the rubber suction pad of the cannon-sight.

'Then do it, damn you!'

The comment died on the moustached Frenchman's lips. Twin puffs of smoke had erupted to the right of the Mark IV's turret. For a moment Bastian was puzzled. A moment later the sudden explosions to his immediate front, followed by a stream of blinding white smoke, enlightened him. The Boche was trying to smother him with a smoke screen. '*Nom de Dieu, Jo-Jo!*' he cried, as the big gunner started to squeeze his ham-fist around the firing lever, 'don't miss the sod the first time!'

'We've done it!' Heinz yelled triumphantly, as the 47mm shell whizzed by the turret harmlessly. 'Heaven, arse and thunderbolt, we've pulled it off, sir!'

'Not quite yet, Heinz,' Kranz replied, pleased all the same that his trick had paid off. 'We've got to *find* the Frog now.'

29

'Easier than pinching pennies from blind school kids,' Heinz said confidently. 'There he is!'

The stab of purple flame through the thick white mass of smoke did indeed pin-point the hidden French tank as well as any marker flare. Kranz could see that. 'All right, then, what are you waiting for, you Bavarian barn-shitter,' he cried exuberantly. 'Sock the bastard for six.'

'With pleasure, the *greatest* pleasure, Major,' Kranz gasped and pulled back the firing lever.

The Mark IV shuddered. Acrid fumes filled the turret. The smoking-yellow shell container rattled to the floor in the same instant that Kurt shot forward again. Tensely Kranz pressed his face to the periscope, feeling its cold metal stick to his sweating forehead. For what seemed an age, nothing happened. Desperately, his eyes searched the white fog for any sign of a hit, while next to him Heinz waited, hand curled round the firing lever.

The Mark IV trembled violently. The white fog was split apart by a great violet flash, followed by dark figures of human beings hurtling through the air. Kranz clapped his hand across Heinz's shoulder. '*You did it . . . You did it!*' He cried, tears of gratitude flooding his grey eyes. 'You got the sod. I'll never say another word against you hairy-assed Bavarians. You can really shoot!'

'Didn't I always tell you, Major? I was William Tell's natural son.' The gunner roared with laughter and pulled the firing lever again.

'Hello, Max . . . hello, Max . . . can you read me?' Kranz cried over the mike. 'Come on in now . . . come to Papa, we've got the Frog bastards by the short and curlies . . . Do you read me?'

'I read you, sir . . . I read you . . . Good shooting, sir!'

'Now good hunting,' Kranz cried, filled with the euphoric blood-lust of battle. 'Let's finish the Frog bastards off. *Now!*'

For a little while the battlefield on the River Meuse was left to the dead, while the exhausted attackers slumped on their haunches in the mud or stretched out full length on the burning decks of their tanks.

They lay everywhere, French and German, entwined like lovers in the promiscuity of death, among the debris of war. Kranz viewed his first battlefield. He had often imagined what it would be like ever since he had been recalled to the *Werhmacht* in August 1939. But his imagination had never reached to this horror. He stared at the bodies everywhere. Khaki and field-grey, they were piled up on all sides like logs of wood. *This* was how human beings, men like himself who had loved and been loved, who had drunk and laughed and had thought in the silliness of their youth that they would live for ever, ended up.

Major Kranz bit his bottom lip and stared down at the mud below the tank. Something glinted dully there. For a moment he thought it might be a piece of looted jewellery. Then with a shudder of horror he recognized it for what it was – a crescent of gleaming white teeth set in the blood-red gore of a shattered jawbone.

'Something run over your grave, sir?' von Fromm's voice enquired.

'No, you louse, just a premonition—' Kranz caught himself in time. He could not tell his second-in-command that he had just had a sudden vision of himself lying there among the dead. It would not do – even for an officer of the reserve.

'Premonition?'

'A sudden chill, von Fromm, that's all.'

Von Fromm, his face still streaked with black powder burns, looked up at him inquiringly, but he said nothing.

For a moment or two the officers said nothing, their attention concentrated on the fresh infantry marching up the bank and forming up to head west, while young infantry officers consulted their maps importantly, field-glasses hanging loose from their necks like third-rate actors in some peacetime war film. More cannonfodder to be thrust into the gory maws of the hungry beast of war waiting for them ahead.

'Well, von Fromm,' Kranz broke the heavy silence, 'what do you think of the Ghost Division now, eh?'

Von Fromm shrugged carelessly. 'It's a fighting unit and it's armoured. I want to know about our Erwin Johannes Eugen Wommel.'

Kranz nodded. 'All I'm sure of is that the man really is a live-wire. He'll be a field-marshal — or dead before this war is over.'

'Let us hope the first alternative is correct, gentlemen,' a Swabian voice broke into their conversation.

The two officers stiffened to attention, but General Rommel grinned and indicated with an urgent wave of his grey-gloved hand that they should relax. 'Never mind military courtesy on a day like this, gentlemen,' he said heartily. 'We have won a victory. Thanks to you, we can relax. After all, you're probably going to have a hard campaign in front of you. You'll need your strength for other things than playing toy soldiers.'

Von Fromm's eyes sparkled. 'You mean we're really going to stay with you, sir?' he exclaimed, forgetting his lisp for a moment in his excitement.

'Yes, Captain. General von Kluge has agreed to allow you to remain temporarily with me. You will make up the losses suffered by my Panzer regiment. When the time comes you will be returned to Army Group.'

'Thank you, sir,' von Fromm breathed and looked at his CO with sparkling eyes.

'Don't thank me too soon, young man,' Rommel replied in high good humour. 'You don't know what the Division's next objective is yet. You might change your mind when you hear it, you know.'

'Never, General,' von Fromm said boldly. 'I thought I was going to stay with the base-stallions for the rest of this war. I'm a regular, sir, and combat is the only way a regular gets promotion — and tin . . .' He tapped his black tunic, bare of any decoration save the Sports Medal in gold, to indicate what he meant. 'The Ghost Division will ensure that I get that combat.'

'It will indeed. And my compliments, young man. That was well spoken.' Rommel beamed at von Fromm. 'You sound like

I did when I was in my twenties, during the last war. It's a simple formula. Battle equals promotion and decorations.'

'And *death*,' Kranz felt like saying. Instead he inquired, 'And what *is* our next objective, General Rommel?'

The Swabian turned his searching blue eyes on the young Major, sweeping his pale, dirty face, as if he were trying to find some sign of fear there. He did not. 'Our next objective?' he echoed Kranz's query. 'Well, it seems that the High Command has gained some confidence in the Ghost Division since we have now successfully cracked the Meuse Line on time.' He shrugged. 'Or, conversely, they think my wooden-headed Thuringians are good at bulling their way through fortified positions. At all events, they have given us another fortified line to break through.' He paused for a fraction of a second, his foxlike face suddenly thoughtful, as if he were, realizing for the first time just what he was about to undertake. The two officers waited expectantly.

'Yes, gentlemen, it will be quite an interesting military exercise. They have given us the Maginot Line to break through . . .' And with that piece of shattering news, General Rommel was gone.

TWO: THE MAGINOT LINE, MAY 15th, 1940

ONE

'The Division will now advance!'

Everywhere the radios crackled, galvanizing the weary, waiting soldiers of the Ghost Division into excited action. Tank motors burst into life. Officers bellowed orders. Red-faced NCOs ran up and down the long columns. The infantry, already laden in the trucks and halftracks, gripped their weapons nervously. This was it!

With a frightening, earth-shaking roar the guns crashed into action. Screaming in hoarse exultation the heavy shells tore over the heads of the Ghost Division men as they started to advance. They ripped the night sky apart, their first angry sighs growing into a baleful howl, mounting in intensity until the bombardment became a monstrous Wagnerian cacophony.

In a flash the first enemy line of defence disappeared. But the tanks were taking no chances. On General Rommel's specific orders, they sprayed the verges and ditches of the road to Avesnes with m.g. fire. No lucky French anti-tank gunner was going to hold up the advance of the Ghost Division this night.

The barrage rolled on ahead of the Division's point. Everywhere the Northern French countryside was lit up by the ugly scarlet flame of bursting shells. A huge explosion and the whole sky to the south was burning a brilliant red. A French Army fuel dump had received a direct hit.

The Division's speed increased. Engines roared. Tank tracks clanked and clattered over the cobbled, dead-straight French roads, as the great divisional box – tanks at the point and flanks, motorized infantry in the centre – moved ever forwards.

The point crossed the railway line south-west of Soire-le-Château and swung onto the main highway, heading for the Maginot Line. The first tank roared into the village. Windows were flung open. Anxious, angry voices yelled startled questions in French. Then the half-naked civilians saw the black and white cross on the side of the vehicles roaring past. '*Les Boches!*' they cried in fear. '*Les Boches sont ici!*'

Everywhere the civilians and the soldiers billeted in the village fled into the fields, as the following tanks began to shoot up their houses. In a matter of moments, the whole village was burning fiercely. Colonel Rothenburg, commander of the 25th Panzer Regiment, nodded his approval and radioed back to the General at Divisional HQ. '*We have broken through. Maginot Line almost ours!*' The Ghost Division rolled on, leaving a burning Soire-le-Château behind it.

Now they were rattling behind their rolling barrage into the heart of the Line, that vaunted French fortification which its creator Maginot had boasted would stop any attacker for a thousand years. Still they had met no opposition. In the cold light of the full moon, there was no sign of the French. Where were their bunkers and pillboxes? Were they underground? Would their guns appear from the earth at the very last moment? At the point the tankers began to grow apprehensive. It was all too easy.

Suddenly scarlet flame stabbed the night. The leading Mark III came to an abrupt stop. For an instant nothing happened. Abruptly its fuel tank exploded. In a flash it was a blazing torch. As if in answer to a command, the whole horizon erupted. From the well-concealed pillboxes on both sides of the highway, the French gunners – hidden deep beneath the earth – fired their automatic cannon. Suddenly the whole of Colonel Rothenburg's point was a blazing chaos of wrecked tanks. The 25th Panzer Regiment had bumped right into the heart of the Maginot defences. The Ghost Division's second battle of the campaign in the West could commence.

As abruptly as it had started, the Divisional barrage ceased. It left behind an echoing silence, which reverberated to and fro between the low hills. In their pillboxes the *chasseurs* waited. Not for long.

A single whistle shrilled. Another followed. And another. In an instant the officers commanding the two attack companies of the 7th Infantry Battalion rose to their feet, yelling their orders. The infantry, heavy packs bumping up and down on their backs, rifles clasped in sweaty hands, lumbered forward over the uneven field. An m.g. opened up, chattering like an angry woodpecker. Men fell heavily. An officer fanned the air with his hands, as if he were attempting to climb an invisible ladder, and pitched forward on his face. His men ran over his dead body. More were hit. Now the cry *'Stretcher-bearers forward . . . Stretcher-bearers at the double!'* went up on all sides.

Within minutes the two attack companies were reduced to little groups of frightened men, springing from hole to hole, as French m.g. fire zipped at them from all sides, dropping in sudden panic as the white tracer cut the air at waist-height, scything down everything in its path.

'Grenades . . . use your grenades, you idiots!' a red-faced, angry officer, the blood streaming down the side of his face, yelled. 'Bomb the bastards!'

Kneeling in the shell-holes, the harassed, frightened infantry pulled out the china pins from their heavy stick-grenades and began to lob them at the concealed m.g. pits. The trick worked. At least the exploding grenades rattled the French, blinding them momentarily with their violent scarlet light. The infantry stumbled forward again.

They hit a trench line. Swarthy French faces under black berets stared up at them in terror. The mud-splattered, bloody German infantry ran at them with the bayonet, all their pent-up rage bursting forth. Like a pack of wild animals they slashed, hacked, sliced, gouged the *chasseurs,* slaughtering them without mercy. Bayonets were torn out of their hands. They used their cruel, studded boots. Their bloody fingers grabbed for French throats. Baying like crazed hounds, they swayed back and forth, locked in individual combat, smashing their boots into one another's genitals, gouging out each other's eyes, ripping open nostrils, their blood and vomit streaming down their uniforms unnoticed, dying together, clinging to one another like lovers exhausted by the strength of their love.

And then the survivors were through the *chasseurs,* running heavily for the bunkers, led by the only surviving officer, his sole weapon a shovel, dripping with gore. Perhaps the young lieutenant saw himself as another Brandt of Fort Douaumont.[1] No one ever knew, for the officer had only another fifteen minutes to live. At all events, crying wildly, he led the handful of survivors directly into the minefield.

They clambered over the rusty barbed wire and put their boots down — right on to the plungers. A soldier screamed as the first mine exploded underneath him, ripping away most of his lower body, leaving him to stare — for one long last moment — at his legs lying five metres away. Another mine exploded. But the young officer seemed to possess a charmed life. He zig-zagged towards the great grey concrete bunker, waving his bloody spade, crying, '*Follow me . . . follow me, men!*' while his command died behind him, littering the French earth with their hideously mutilated bodies. Finally an unknown *chasseur* took pity on him. Standing at the door of the latrine to which he had gone to relieve himself, his flies still unbuttoned, he raised his rifle in the cold, cruel light of the moon, and took careful aim. As if he were on the range back at Verdun, he remembered to breathe easily and squeeze, not clutch the trigger. The rifle butt slapped his shoulder satisfactorily. Fifty metres away the Boche stopped, as if he had suddenly run into a brick wall. For a moment he swayed there, alone and dying, seemingly attempting to come to some overwhelming decision, his young face frowning the way children frown. Then the blood poured out of his mouth in a great crimson flood and he slammed to the earth.

[1] A young lieutenant who conquered the famous French fort at Verdun in 1916 and thereafter became a celebrated hero at the Imperial Court.

TWO

'*General, they have brought us to a standstill. Two infantry companies gone. Over.*' Colonel von Bismarck dabbed his brow with a cologne-scented lace handkerchief.

'*No panic?*' Rommel's coarse Swabian voice crackled metallically over the ether. '*Over.*'

'*No panic, General. Over.*'

'*What is your plan? Over.*'

Colonel von Bismarck caught his biting comment just in time. The Swabian peasant was impossible. He saw just glory. He, von Bismarck, saw dead men, German soldiers, fathers and lovers and sons who would be sorely missed in their Thuringian hill-villages. How could one plan an attack on a fortified line with tanks and infantry? One needed cannon, really heavy cannon. Why, in the war he had fought in on this very spot 22 years before, they had used 420mm howitzers, manned by whole artillery companies, to reduce the French fortifications. He swallowed his rage. '*I plan to contain them with infantry, General, and then see if I can outflank them.*'

'*Impossible!*' Rommel said bluntly. '*It will completely upset my timetable. The* Führer *would not like it. Alternative plan please? Over.*'

'*Alternative . . . General Rommel?*' von Bismarck said, forcing himself to be calm. '*You have not seen what we are faced with. Even the well-known bravery of the German soldier—*'

'*I don't want excuses, Bismarck,*' Rommel cut him short, abandoning radio procedure. '*I want positive suggestions on how we are to solve the present problem.*'

'*Good, then you shall have them!*' Colonel von Bismarck cried with a trace of that monumental anger which had motivated his great ancestor 'the Iron Chancellor'. '*Give me guns — big, heavy guns — and I'll crack this particular nut for you, General Rommel. Over and out.*'

The infantry commander slammed the radio phone back down into its cradle and barked at the startled radio operator, 'Listen, I'm not available to anyone now for the next two hours, even if the Lord God himself calls me up. Understood?'

'Understood, *Herr Oberst*,' the young operator stuttered. 'But—'

But Colonel von Bismarck, his face crimson with rage, had already stalked out.

With its usual maddening slowness, dawn came. Captain Gehendges yawned yet once again and shuddered a little with the night cold. He ached everywhere from sleeping on the hard French ground next to the battery and he longed for a cigarette. But Division Regulations were no naked lights during the hours of darkness, and Captain Gerhardt Gehendges had always been a stickler for rules and regulations.

Gloomily the commander of the 25th Panzer Regiment's flak battery wiped his gold-rimmed pince-nez clean and stared down at his well-manicured hands, now filthy and unwashed since the previous morning. He shuddered and wished he was back with his ample-bosomed 'little Mother', as he called his wife Anna, enjoying the fresh rolls and coffee in their little house on the outskirts of Cologne.

Six months before, when he had been called back to the *Wehrmacht* as a 40-year-old reserve officer, he had been overjoyed. For 21 years since he had returned from France, a young infantry lieutenant, in 1918, he had followed his career as an insurance salesman with the *Colonia* dutifully. Anna, the twins, the suburban house with its neat garden, the slow promotion at work, the routine of his daily contacts, 'Good morning, gracious lady, I'm from the *Colonia*. I hear that you wish to insure your house, your husband, your car . . .' Year in, year out, he had been a good husband and a good provider, growing portly, short-sighted and balding, all the time thrusting those desires of the flesh and spirit which plagued him into the back of his mind, as unworthy of the acting assistant insurance sales manager at *Colonia AG*.

The day he had been recalled, however, patting his motherly wife's shoulder sympathetically while she sobbed, he had a sudden vision of freedom again. His mind had filled with himself as a young lieutenant of infantry once more, the fire and fury of that smooth-faced youth's life: champagne out of women's shoes and giggling, half-naked whores in sheer black silk stockings. With the recall-telegram clutched in his pudgy hand, he told himself almost guiltily, 'It's my *last* chance.' Now, half a year later as the head of a flak battery, he had dragged his 88mm monsters across Poland without having fired a shot. Belgium had been the same. Once they had spotted a Tommy plane, but it had got away before they had even loaded. France, seemingly, was going to be different.

Gloomily Captain Gehendges tweaked the dew-drop off the end of his nose and told himself he might as well be back with 'little Mother' and the *Colonia*. His guns had remained as virginal as he was. In this war there was a shortage of both giggling half-naked whores in sheer black silk stockings and enemy to fight, or so it seemed.

Now the horizon was beginning to break up and already his gunners were beginning to rise from their damp blankets and urinate in hot steaming gushes against the side of their 88mms. Gehendges told himself he could risk a cigarette.

He sat on an ammunition box, smoking cigarette after cigarette, refusing the sausage sandwich the cook brought him, sipping his ersatz coffee morosely, contemplating the start of another day which would undoubtedly be as routine and as dull for Flak Battery 6 as the one before had been. Sunk in his own gloomy reverie, he did not hear the soft squeak of the car brakes, nor the suddenly excited whisper of his men, not even the firm confident tread of highly polished boots behind him. But the first words of the man, who would very shortly be the cause of *Hauptmann* Gerhardt Gehendges's death, told the middle-aged Captain, without having to look round, that he was in the presence of authority. 'Captain,' the Swabian-accented voice barked, 'tell me what is the exact penetration of your cannon?'

Captain Gehendges sprang to his feet more quickly than if a

whole host of the half-naked whores he dreamed about at night had suddenly appeared out of nowhere. He clicked to attention and nearly let his pince-nez drop. It was the General – General Erwin Rommel, the divisional commander!

'Sir?' he queried absurdly.

Rommel, his foxlike face as keen as ever in spite of the earliness of the hour, repeated his question, a sudden impatient look in his bright blue eyes.

'Don't know, sir,' Gehendges stuttered, feeling a fool. 'No one has ever worked it out. You see, General, the skin of the average plane is thin enough to be penetrated by a 9mm bullet. The 88mm's penetration power has not been regarded as important, only its range.'

Rommel nodded his understanding. 'I see, Captain, but you do know its muzzle velocity?'

Gehendges suppressed a sigh of relief quickly. That he *did* know. 'Yessir, one thousand metres per second.'

'And the weight of a round?'

'Ten and a half kilos, sir,' Gehendges repeated dutifully, wondering what all this was leading to, and hoping that by the time the General got round to inspecting his battery, which was obviously his reason for being here at this ungodly hour, the sergeant-major would have got the men washed and tidied up a bit. Otherwise there would be hell to pay. Rommel was famous – infamous would be a better word – for his temper if his soldiers did not meet up to his own high standards of discipline and turnout.

But Rommel had not come to pay a visit to the obscure little anti-aircraft battery. He had other plans for Captain of the Reserves Gerhardt Gehendges. Finishing his rapid calculations, he said, 'As you perhaps know, Captain, your regiment has been stalled up there at the Maginot Line. The French's faith in concrete has paid off – for the time being. The guns in those casemates of theirs can penetrate the armour of both the Mark III and IV, I'm very much afraid.'

'I see, sir,' Gehendges answered routinely, not seeing at all, wondering what all this talk was leading up to.

44

'However, Captain, offensive is always superior to defensive. Besides, there are serious defects in the lay-out of the line, as I have seen this dawn. Insufficient attention has been paid to the need for the fire from the various forts to be interlocking. Knock out one or two of them and the way is open. The rest can be left to rot for all I'm concerned.' He smiled bleakly at the now completely bewildered Captain. 'But first we have to knock out those couple of forts, haven't we?'

'Yessir.'

'Now, I've been told by Intelligence that the concrete of the casemates is about three metres thick. With your shell weight and muzzle velocity, I should think it would be possible to penetrate that concrete at a range of — say — one hundred to one hundred and fifty metres. What do you think?'

Gerhardt Gehendges gulped. 'But we're anti-aircraft gunners, General,' he protested. 'I know nothing about using the 88mm as field artillery.'

'Well, my dear Captain, now you must learn, must you not?' Rommel's voice was suddenly harsh and incisive. 'Report immediately to Colonel von Bismarck. He will arrange every-thing. You will begin your attack at ten hundred hours. Good morning.'

'Good morning, sir,' Gehendges answered in a sinking voice.

Captain Gehendges's memory of the First World War told him Colonel von Bismarck had almost reached breakpoint. The elderly Colonel's hands trembled as he marked in the enemy positions with the china pencil and at every opportunity he took a deep drag at his cigarette, as if his very life depended upon it. Whenever the cannon thundered from the French positions, he jumped like some wet-tailed greenhorn on his first day at the front. All the same, his exposé was clear and detailed. 'In short, Captain,' he summed up for the apprehensive Gehendges, who had by now realized what he was letting himself in for, 'we feel, the General and I, that if we knock out bunkers A and B, which as you can see cover the main road to Avesnes, via the village of Semousies, we'll be able to move on without bothering to take

45

the other bunkers of this sector of the line.' He took another deep gratifying drag of his cigarette. 'There are two flies in the ointment, however. The one, I've told you about. Bunker A can cover Bunker B and vice-versa. You will therefore be under enemy shellfire once you get within range.'

'I understand, Colonel,' Gehendges said, realizing suddenly he should have stayed in Cologne. Damn the giggling whores in black silk stockings; he just was not cut out to be a hero. 'And the other, Colonel?' he prompted.

Von Bismarck frowned, thinking of the two companies of infantry he had lost in such a terrible manner that dawn. 'Mines,' he answered grimly. 'The fields in front of the two bunkers are infested with mines, both anti-personnel and,' he hesitated, 'I'm afraid, anti-vehicle, too.'

Gehendges said nothing. He could not. Like a lamb being led to the slaughter, he let his hand be shook, his shoulder patted sympathetically and his car be summoned to drive him away. Captain Gehendges's short and unhappy war had begun.

THREE

'*Oh, I'll stroke my hairy arse,*' Sergeant-Major Schott exploded, his red, good-humoured face for once apprehensive, as he and Gehendges viewed the scene in front of them. 'Not only are we supposed to become field gunners, the General's also expecting us to become knobble-kneed shitting stubble-hoppers. Those are *mines* out there, Captain.'

Miserably, Captain Gehendges nodded his agreement. 'I thought I wouldn't tell the men until we arrived at the scene of the action,' he said.

'How right you are, sir,' Schott said, tipping his helmet to the back of his broad shaven head. 'That bunch of sugar-tits who are presently masquerading as gunners would fill their lace drawers straight off. You have my word on that.'

Gehendges knew well what the big blunt Berlin NCO, who had once been a socialist trade union leader in the middle-thirties before he disappeared into the Army in order to escape being placed in a prison or worse, was right. Most of his men were over-age retreads from the First World War, like himself, or younger men, unfit to serve as infantry or tankers, plus a few dodgers who had worked out that flak was a cushy number.

He stared at the shattered landscape ahead, littered with what looked like bundles of rags, which had once been men, sprawled over the rusting barbed wire, surrounded by the bloody bits of what was left of their limbs. Then he turned to the far distance, at the low threatening outlines of the French forts. 'I'll tell you one thing, sir, for free. We'll never make it — not with that lot and under these conditions. Try clearing those mines and there's gonna be a lot of singing tenors among the greenhorns.'

'But there must be a way, Sergeant-Major,' Gehendges said miserably. 'There must!'

'I know, sir, I know. The big animals are after your arse —

excuse my High German. You lose both ways — if you try, or if you don't try.'

Gehendges nodded and wrung his pudgy hands. 'What are we going to do?'

Schott looked at him calculatingly. He knew his Gehendges. There were millions of them in the Third Reich: middle-aged family-fathers with little houses who had voted for Hitler in 1933 so that they could go on living the way they had always lived. The Gehendgeses of this world lived for security, even if that security was provided by Hitler and his gangsters. All the same, the Old Man was not a bad sort and besides he did not want Gehendges risking the men's lives in some impossible adventure. No, he would not tolerate that.

'Listen, sir,' he began slowly, his mind made up. 'Between us nuns, I think I could help if you could be persuaded to help me. You know what they say, Captain, one hand washes the other?'

Hope leapt up in Gehendges's watery eyes. 'How do you mean, Schott?' he asked quickly.

'Well, sir, if a certain Sergeant-Major Schott could be allowed to go on emergency leave to Berlin to visit his little wifey at the end of this campaign — for, say, eight days — although there is no emergency, that certain Sergeant-Major might be able to figure out a way to get the battery across that minefield within good range of those Frog bunkers.'

'Anything . . . anything. I promise you *anything*,' Gehendges said excitedly, clutching at straws. 'You have my word as a German officer, Schott.'

'I'd rather have a packet of cancer-sticks,' Schott told himself, but to the officer he said, 'All right, sir, if you would be so kind as to nip across to that tank squadron over there and see if you can get their officer to give us some covering smoke, I'll go and collect the men's toothpowder and we'll get on with it.'

'*Toothpowder* . . . *we?*' Gehendges stuttered in puzzled apprehension. 'I don't understand.'

Schott grinned at him. 'You don't have to, sir. You're an officer and a gentleman. Now the smoke, if you please, sir . . .'

Major Kranz raised his right hand and flung a quick glance to left and right. His tanks were drawn up in a long line in the dead ground, which the French gunners would not be able to reach, and their mortar fire would have little effect on the Mark IV's half-metre-thick armour. Everywhere the gunners were in position behind their guns, already loaded with smoke shells. He hesitated for an instant. He had not thought the fat artillery captain who had come pleading for his help had this kind of courage in him. He had looked a typical base-stallion. But there he was positioned behind the wheel of the big towing vehicle, with an 88mm flak cannon attached to it.

Kranz licked his lips. He only hoped his gunners would ration out their smoke shells until the fat Captain was within range, as he had ordered them to do. There were only six smoke shells per tank and with the light breeze that was blowing from the south-west, the smoke screen would soon dissipate. Once the big towing vehicle was caught out in the open, the French gunners would blast it to hell and back within an instant. He brought his right hand down sharply. It was the signal. '*Fire!*' he bellowed in the same moment that the fourteen 75mm cannon burst into life.

One moment later the first smoke shells began to burst in a sudden spurt of thick white smoke one hundred metres ahead of the towing vehicle.

Sergeant-Major Schott, crouched fifty metres ahead of the vehicle, moved for the first time in an hour. For the last sixty minutes he had been part of the tableau of death: the waxen-faced group of infantry who had been caught in the first burst of m.g. fire the previous night, the flies already crawling over their glazed, unseeing eyes, stinking now as they huddled there like rotting cabbage stumps in some abandoned Berlin allotment. But he still did not rise to his feet. The French observers some three hundred metres away, peering over the blasted cicatrized landscape might well yet see him. The smoke screen was still not thick enough for him. Sergeant-Major Schott waited patiently, because Sergeant-Major Schott was going to survive this war; he would not die for Hitler and his gang.

Now the white wall was thick enough for him. Tapping his belt to check that the bundles of stick grenades were in place and that the flap of his pistol holster was open ready for instant action, the big Berliner rose to his feet and stole forward, starting to lay the trail of tooth powder behind him. To his rear he heard Gehendges start up the towing vehicle's motor. In spite of his own danger, Schott grinned. He could imagine the Old Man was pissing down his left leg with fear by now; and by the time he had cleared the minefield — *if he did* — his whole plumbing system would be working overtime.

Schott dismissed the Captain, concentrating now on his task. As he anticipated, it was not too difficult. The dead bodies, horribly maimed and mutilated, indicated well enough where the mines were. The trouble would start where he ran out of dead bodies.

Time passed leadenly. The only noise now was his own harsh breathing, the rumble of the big truck to his rear and regular soft plop of the exploding smoke shells. Twice he spotted the deadly prongs of an anti-vehicle mine and carefully drew a trail of white tooth powder round them, hoping that the Frogs hadn't played any tricks, like attaching another mine to them at an irregular distance. But Schott reasoned, soldiers were the same the whole world over: order and regularity dominated their lives. The minefield had probably been laid according to some plan drawn up by the French War Ministry a hundred years before. He hoped so. He crawled on.

Fifty metres . . . one hundred metres . . . one hundred and fifty metres . . . two hundred metres . . . The bodies were beginning to peter out now. He was almost there . . . *Two hundred and twenty-five metres . . .* The dead body of a lone officer, a neat hole drilled with crimson precision right in the middle of his forehead, and the toothpowder had given out!

For a moment Schott crouched, breathing as if he had just run a hard race, his broad, honest red face glazed with sweat. Fear swept through him for an instant as he realized just how

50

suicidal his position was: in the middle of nowhere, with the rest of a minefield to contend with and half the French army within spitting distance. He must not have had all his cups in his cupboard to have volunteered for a damn fool mission like this. Then he pulled himself together. He tugged the roll of personal lavatory paper out of his back pocket, remembering a lecture to his gunners: 'As senior NCO, I demand my own thunderbox and the luxury of real craphouse paper on my lily-white sergeant-major's bottom — and woe betide any of you turnip-heads I find sneaking into my crapper!' Now he started crawling forward once more, trailing the dull white roll of paper behind him, praying that the breeze would not blow it away, his keen eyes searching the debris-littered field ahead of him apprehensively for the deadly spikes and hooks.

Twice he nearly put his hands on anti-personnel mines, the sweat now dripping from his bushy eyebrows blinding him to the danger almost until the very last moment. He gulped and crawled on. Then he was at the start of a rusting wire barrier and he knew he was through. The Frogs would not lay mines uselessly among wire, he reasoned. Apart from that, the wire barrier indicated that the bunker was close by. He breathed out a fervent sigh of relief. He had done it! All that was needed now was for Captain Gehendges to get his fat Cologne arse up here before the smoke screen cleared!

It was then that it happened. The all-concealing screen drifted away and Schott was staring up at the massive outline of the bunker only one hundred metres away, feeling absurdly naked and foolish, like a latterday David about to tackle some monstrous Goliath.

'*Tit and turd!*' Kranz cursed, spotting the danger at once, 'it's clearing too soon. Gunner! Have you got another smoke round left?'

'No, sir,' the gunner gasped anxiously. Kranz pressed the mike switch. 'Von Fromm, have you smoke?'

'I beg your pardon, sir—'

51

'Don't shit me, von Fromm!' he interrupted angrily. 'No time for games. Have you smoke?'

'One round, sir,' von Fromm's voice was now businesslike and urgent.

'Then in the devil's name plant it between the bunker and that artillery truck or that fat Captain is not going to be with us much longer.'

'Will do, sir. *At the double!*'

Captain Gehendges was preparing for his last manoeuvre – a quick swing round of the big truck so that the 88mm would be facing front and he and Schott could handle it alone in the place of the usual five-man crew – when his horrified gaze saw the smoke begin to disappear and the fort loom up like a great ship glimpsed through fog. '*Oh, my holy strawsack!*' he gulped and almost let go of the wheel in his terror. He seemed almost able to touch the place; it was so close.

For a moment he lost his head. He let go of the accelerator. The truck bucked under him and came to an abrupt stop. He had stalled the motor. *Stalled the motor – here!* a terrified voice within him cried. *Here!*

Schott's broad sturdy figure appeared out of nowhere uniform covered in mud, sweat pouring down his face. 'Man,' he yelled up furiously at the panic-stricken Captain, tears trickling down his ashen, pudgy face, 'don't screw up now! Get on the stick. Start up and turn around—'

His order was drowned by the sudden whine of a slug. The windscreen shattered into a glittering spider's web of smashed glass. Schott spun round. Without appearing to aim, firing from the hip, he felled the bereted *chasseur* who had shot. The man fell screaming over the rusty wire. But there were more of them, doubling forward towards them, yelling as they came, and to their rear, a submerged, snub-nosed 75mm had appeared as if from nowhere and was now beginning to turn in their direction.

'Now the crap has really hit the cookhouse!' Schott exploded, angry that after the effort, the plan was going wrong. He pulled out a stick grenade and tugged out the pin with a quick bite of his teeth. Grunting fiercely, he lobbed it at the yelling Frenchmen. It exploded right among them. Bodies flew to all sides. Suddenly the morning air was loud with their screams. But there were still more of them, confident that they could easily take these two lone Boche who had appeared so abruptly from nowhere. They started to spread out to each flank, firing and dropping, rising, firing and dropping again.

Now, while Gehendges fumbled frantically with the starter, slugs began to whine off the cab and rear of the truck frighteningly. Schott dropped to his knees, pistol in one hand, grenade hanging by its pin from his teeth. If he were going to go hop on this one, he told himself, he was going to take a shitting lot of frog-eaters with him.

'*Merde! Allez!*' a French voice cried to Schott's right. He did not understand the words, but the tone sufficed. They were attacking. He swung round. A little bunch of *chasseurs*, screaming their heads off, were rushing forward with fixed bayonets. He loosed off three single shots. Three *chasseurs* went down. He ripped the pin out of the grenade and threw it. Its blast swept another four away, leaving them broken-limbed and dying in the steaming fresh brown pit. But there were two of them still determined to stick their bayonets in the Boche. Schott pressed the trigger of his pistol. Nothing happened! He had committed the cardinal mistake. He had not changed the magazine in time. He flung the useless thing away angrily. The Frenchmen saw the gesture. They laughed triumphantly and came in for the kill.

A big one, face wolfish and unshaven under the overlarge, floppy black beret, lunged. Schott dodged just in time. The bayonet rammed uselessly into the door of the cab. A second later, Schott's cruelly nailed boot lashed out and caught the unsuspecting Frenchman on his shin. He went down with a howl of pain to receive the stamp of Schott's other boot on his unshaven jaw. It cracked underfoot like a walnut shell. Schott yelped with pain. The man's bayonet had gone right through his left arm, pinning him against the side of the truck.

Schott caught a glimpse of an evil, triumphant face, distorted

53

by the lust to kill. He fought down his panic, trying to outreason the confident Frenchman as he took a deep breath and prepared to withdraw his bloody bayonet for the final kill. Grinding his teeth together against the pain, Schott beat him to it, turning his body to the left, feeling the keen blade bite ever deeper, but knowing that in this way he would prevent the Frog from withdrawing the bayonet. Now he knew he must act fast. Standard bayonet fighting technique in a situation like this was to pull the trigger and blow the blade free. Schott was not going to give the Frog that chance.

With his back half-turned to the Frenchman, he lashed out with his heel. Luck was with him. The metal-plated heel caught the unsuspecting *chasseur* right in the crotch. He went down screaming, leaving the bayonet plunged deep in Schott's shoulder. The big NCO did not hesitate. With his right hand he heaved. The blade came out in a gush of blood, with his own piteous scream of self-pity. For a moment he slumped there, faint and weak, watching the Frenchman writhing on the ground, hands clasped fervently to his injured crotch. With the last of his strength he forced himself to pick up the bayonet, wait till the Frenchman presented his back to him and then, in the same instant that Gehendges finally managed to get the motor started, he plunged it home savagely.

FOUR

The thick white smoke streamed from von Fromm's last shell, directly between the two men frantically manoeuvring the big gun, and the stubby French cupola gun swinging round in their direction. Kranz yelled a hasty congratulation to von Fromm and added, 'Take over here, von Fromm. I'm going to get the rest of those artillery men moving. They'll need another gun up there soon.'

'And the Guard?' von Fromm asked.

Kranz's reply was unprintable. 'Driver,' he commanded hastily, 'get the lead out of your tail! Over we go to the flak boys and put some pepper up their asses.'

'Yessir,' Kurt sang out and pressed the starter in that same moment that a shaking Gerhardt Gehendges flung himself behind the sights of the big gun and began frantically whirling the wheels to bring the long, menacing barrel down to point at the still hidden fort, while a bleeding Schott thrust home the first ten-kilo shell.

Firing blind, but knowing that he could not miss at this range, and also that he must begin his attack before the smoke cleared, Gehendges pulled the firing lever. The huge gun erupted into earth-shaking life. The air was ripped apart with the sound like that of a gigantic piece of canvas being torn open, and the first shell was hissing towards the French fort.

The fort seemed to heave like a live thing under the impact. Dust rained down on the defenders and the corridors were suddenly flooded with a biting stink of high explosive. The lights flickered, went out, and then on again, but this time a dim yellow. The first Boche shell had struck lucky. It must have hit the main power plant. They were on emergency already.

Capitaine LeGrand looked at the faces of his staff, young Lieutenant Doux and Sergeant-Major Driant, a veteran of Verdun in 1916. They seemed suddenly to be smeared with grease – and he knew why. The two of them were scared. He slapped his cane against his immaculate riding boot, above the elegant hand-cut riding breeches, and spoke easily, 'Just carry on routinely. There is no need for panic. We are quite safe here against everything the gentlemen from the other side can throw at us. Driant, check they have got the smoke ejectors.'

Another thunderous blow rocked the fort and he had to grab onto the metal table secured to the floor to prevent himself from falling but LeGrand went on, 'And you, Doux, get up into the top gallery and see if you can't draw a bead on them. Off you go now like good chaps.'

Like 'good chaps' they went, and LeGrand breathed out hard, allowing the fear he could not show in front of his subordinates to appear in his dark, liquid eyes. That morning when they had stopped the Boche infantry attack so easily, he had felt very safe behind his three metres of concrete; now that same concrete gave him a sense of being trapped – a sardine in a can which could be opened up at any moment. He looked at the notice he had pinned up on the wall of the control room. It was the proud motto from Fort Douaumont in 1916. 'RATHER BE BURIED UNDER THE RUINS OF THE FORT THAN SURRENDER!' He knew it should give him confidence, but it did not. Instead, the thought of being buried alive terrified him.

Another shell slammed into the side of the fort and again the control room was flooded with the burning stench of HE. Somewhere down the corridor a soldier started to scream hysterically, until the sound of a slap and a brutal curse in Provençal patois silenced the man. LeGrand grabbed for the phone. 'Doux, are you up there?' He did not wait for the Lieutenant's reply. 'What does it look like outside?'

'I don't know, *mon capitaine*,' Doux gasped.

'What do you mean, you young idiot?'

'Sir, the observation post has been hit. We're blinded.'

'How can we be? What about the gunners in the front turret?'

Doux almost let his fear overwhelm him – he could already sense the catastrophe which was going to take place here – but he caught himself just in time as a graduate of St Cyr, whose family had served in the armies of France since the days of Napoleon, should. 'They refuse to enter the turret, sir.'

'*What?*' LeGrand exploded.

'Yessir. They say the Boche gun is aimed straight for them. It's suicide to open fire on him. They say the Boche should be allowed to think they've knocked out gun number one.'

'Why this is mutiny, Doux! What did you say? What did you do, eh?'

'I didn't know what to do, sir. I thought—'

LeGrand gave him no further opportunity to explain. The rot had begun already. This might well be Verdun all over again. Hastily he grabbed his pistol belt and strapped it on. With his riding cane in his hand, he doubled out of the command post. Men were already crowding the dim corridor, their faces grey with fear, their eyes wild, wide and staring. He opened his mouth to shout at them, but the shell beat him to it.

It whacked into the fort, making the whole place tremble. Again the lights flickered and men screamed as the dust came flooding down like a grey snow storm. LeGrand swallowed hard and began hitting them with his cane like an enraged schoolmaster. 'Get back to your posts, you pigs!' he screamed. 'Back to your posts, or I'll shoot you myself!' With all his strength he waded into them, slashing right and left, noting that there were NCOs among the waverers, too. 'Well,' he bellowed, pulling out his pistol, 'who is going to be the first for a bullet?'

The gesture did the trick. Like grey sewer rats they slunk away out of his path, but he knew that once he was gone, they would come back to the safety of the deepest corridor. He strode towards the lift cage and pressed the button. Nothing happened. 'Damn, damn, *damn!*' he cursed. As he had always predicted to the inspecting engineers before the war, the emergency power system would not be strong enough to run the lifts and ammunition hoists. But that was water under the bridge. No time to moralize about it now. Two at a time he took the concrete steps and doubled down to the main turret. He swung round the anti-blast bend and saw the gunners. They were huddled against the dark walls, hands clasped to their ears like frightened children, trying to blot out the noise that frightened them, some of them sobbing hysterically, others twitching like congenital idiots. The sight enraged him beyond measure. He ran at them, slashing their faces or bent backs, crying, '*You sons-of-whores, you turds, get back to your gun—*'

The shell struck the turret directly at the aperture. The 75mm disappeared in a burst of bright scarlet flame which momentarily blinded LeGrand. He was slammed against the wall, as if by a gigantic fist. Hot acrid air flushed down the corridor. Shrapnel howled from wall to wall. Men went down screaming piteously, arms and legs sliced off by the shining, red-hot metal. Suddenly LeGrand found himself swamped in dead and dying men. Groggily he clawed himself free, still unable to see correctly but knowing instinctively that his own fort was powerless to stop the Germans now. Swaying from side to side, bright red stars exploding in front of his eyes, he felt his way back down to the control room, stumbling and falling over prostrate bodies — whether they were dead or alive he did not know, nor did he care. There was only one more thing for him to do in this life — and he was going to do it. Ears singing, the objects around him swaying as if seen through the heat-laden fumes of the African desert where he had learnt his craft, he managed nonetheless to call the support bunker. 'Joubert, Joubert,' he called desperately, forgetting all radio procedure now. 'We're about knocked out. But we'll stick at it. The first Boche you see on my roof, let him have it with all you've got and forget about us. We'll be glad to die for France.'

He let the phone slip out of a nerveless hand.

'*But LeGrand, that's suicide . . . do you hear, LeGrand — suicide . . .*' the faint metallic voice at the other end was squawking, but LeGrand was past caring. Placing his pistol in his mouth, instinctively gagging at its gun-metal, oily taste, he pulled the trigger, spraying that once proud motto with his own gore.

Kranz's tank came to a halt just behind the two 88mms which

were slamming shell after shell into the fort, its side now scarred with shell holes like the symptoms of some loathsome skin disease. Swiftly, Colonel von Bismarck's infantrymen, whom he had 'borrowed', dropped off and buried themselves in the nearest shell holes.

Kranz heaved himself out of the turret after them, crying, 'Heinz, fire in support of the big fellows. You won't do much good, but it'll keep the infantry's spirits up – for a while at least.' Swiftly, doubled low, he ran over to Captain Gehendges and his Sergeant-Major, a big cheeky-looking rogue, a thick blood-stained bandage tied roughly round his arm, from which the blood still trickled down the torn sleeve. 'You'd better get that seen to,' he said as he squatted next to the pudgy Captain.

''Aint even worth talking about, Major,' the big rogue said insolently. 'I've had worse cuts shaving when I've been out on the sauce the night before.'

'That's your funeral then, Sergeant-Major.'

'Don't talk about funerals,' Gehendges quavered. *'Please!'*

Kranz grinned in spite of the racket and the seriousness of the situation. 'Listen, Captain, you're doing a nice job here, but the General wants the operation speeded up.'

'What?'

'No, not you,' Kranz soothed him at once. 'You're to keep on firing, but I'm to take in a bunch of infantry and see if we can't get in at the back door. All you are expected to do is to effectively mask the fort while we try to find the entrance.'

'Oh, thank God for that!' Gehendges breathed, and added hastily, *'Of* course, we would have been prepared to go in, too, but after all, we are specialists, aren't we. Gunners, you know.'

The big, wounded Sergeant-Major winked at the Major over Gehendges's fat shoulder.

'Of course, of course,' Kranz agreed hastily. 'Can't waste your chaps on a routine stubble-hopper operation like this, can we now?'

'You said entrance, sir,' Schott said. 'Well, I don't know where the real one is, but we've made a really nice little hole just up there beyond the front turret. If we could—'

'Of course.' Kranz was quicker. 'Up into the blind ground, onto the roof and down into that hole. That's it. Well,' he raised his voice above the racket, 'what are we waiting for, you infantry? You don't want to live for ever, do you, you dogs?'

Engines going all out, the Mark IV, laden with infantrymen, burst from the cover of the dead land to the right of the crumbling bunker and rocketed across the shell-pitted ground. Behind it the two flak guns thumped away, breaking huge lumps of concrete off the fort with each shell.

For a moment *Commandant* Joubert, peering at the metal monster from the slit in his bunker's observation post, could not make out what the Boche intended. Was he going to ram poor dead LeGrand's bunker? Then he understood. Its tracks whirling furiously, sending up a shower of debris and concrete rubble, the enemy tank ran at the sloped earth which covered the rear wall of the bunker as camouflage. *Naturally*, the Boche commander was going to deliver his infantry onto the roof that way!

Joubert grabbed his mike. 'Listen A Turret. As soon as you see a Boche tank on the other bunker − yes, you've heard me correctly, a *Boche* tank − let it have a salvo. You've got to knock the thing out at once. Understood?'

'Understood,' the faint metallic voice replied.

'Good, then don't fail me, boys!'

Kurt ran through the Mark IV's gears like an artist, foot clamped full down on the accelerator, sliding the gear lever across the bar down into yet another and lower gear immediately the engine roar started to weaken. Like a fly clinging to a ceiling, the 20-ton monster crawled up the 45-degree incline, while Kranz in the turret and the infantry crouched on its burning deck held their breath, visibly willing it to reach the top. Kurst smashed home the lowest gear. The engines were running red-hot now. In the driver's compartment he could feel his feet burning and the sweat had soaked his overalls. '*Come on, you bitch . . . come on, give to Daddy!*' he urged, his eyes fixed hypnotically through the narrow slit on the top of the bunker, which seemed so near and yet so far.

Machine-gun fire came from close by. Kurt ignored it. He had eyes only for the edge. If the motor stalled now, he and the rest of them would be only fit for mincemeat. There was a drop of at least ten metres below them. Thick smoke filled the compartment. He coughed hoarsely. The engine was singing out in wild protest. It might explode at any moment. *'Please . . . please . . . please!'* He pleaded with it as if it were a live thing.

With one last roar, it was over the top and had come to a violent stop on the edge of the bunker, engine blown out. Kurt did not care. He slumped back in his soaked leather seat, all strength gone, ignoring the winking red lights which indicated serious trouble. He had done it!

'Good work, Kurt. You'll get a medal for this,' Major Kranz's voice sang out over the intercom.

'A nice cold beer would be better.'

'I'll buy you a barrel when we're out of here, Kurt.' Kranz, pistol in hand, sprang down from the turret, following the infantry. 'Heinz, keep your eyes skinned—'

A tremendous whoosh cut his words short. Three hundred metres away a blinding light flashed towards them.

'Take cover!' someone screamed in the same moment that the 75mm shell struck the stranded Mark IV directly in its glacis plate. It reared back on its back sprockets like a wild animal, the springs protesting with a loud metallic squeal at the murderous blow, stamping down again with Kurt slumped across the controls, deep purple pits where his eyes had been, and Heinz, his headless body still upright, hands on the firing lever of his gun, a hideous caricature of his former self. An instant later the Mark IV exploded, showering the running infantry with shards of red-hot steel. Men went down screaming everywhere, being swept off the side of the bunker like flies swatted away by some gigantic hand.

Kranz was swept off his feet by the blast. His head cracked the concrete and for a moment he lay there senseless, surrounded by the survivors, while behind them the wrecked Mark IV, possessed of a life of its own, slithered with its dead crew ever closer to the edge of the bunker, until finally it slipped over the side to crash in a mess of rending metal to the earth below.

'Come on, you sons-of-whores!' Schott cried urgently, as he waited for the dark figures lying full length on the roof of the bunker to move. *'Move it!'*

Across at the other bunker, the gun flashed again. A tracer shell whizzed flatly over the intervening space. It exploded only a matter of metres away from the little band of infantry. A dismayed Schott saw how several of them rose into the air and were swept screaming over the side. Still the rest of them did not move.

'What in heaven's name is the matter with them?' Schott screamed. 'Are they tired of living or—'

Again the terrible gun spoke. The bunker trembled as it struck home. German infantry flew over the side. It was too much for Schott.

'Get out of the way,' he yelled, and elbowed the aimer out of his seat behind the sights of the 88mm.

'What are you doing?' Gehendges cried.

'Go and piss in your boot – *sir!*' Schott cried, beside himself with rage, knowing that only he could save the situation now.

'I beg your pardon? Don't you know you are speaking to an officer?' Gehendges blustered.

Schott ignored the pudgy ex-insurance man. Instead he whirled the brass wheels of the gun, as if his very life depended upon it. Now he no longer felt the burning pain in his arm from the bayonet wound. His whole body flooded with frantic energy. He must mask that Frog gun!

The round turret of the other bunker slid into the bright calibrated sight. Solid metal, he recognized it immediately. He did not have a chance in hell of penetrating it, and at that range there was no hope of a lucky shot penetrating the aperture, as had been the case with the first bunker. He pressed his right eyes to the rubber suction pad, making a quick decision. Below would not affect the Frog crew. But above might just chip off enough concrete and shake loose enough dust within the chamber to unsettle them. Hardly daring to breathe, he squeezed the firing bar.

The 88mm erupted with a tremendous crash. At the other side of the gun, the layer grunted as he lifted the next shell to be inserted. Schott glued his eye to the sight. The spent cartridge ejected itself with a blast of acrid air, which slapped the big NCO across the face like a blow. He blinked and flashed his eyes open again. The shell exploded in a thick spurt of violet light and dust directly above the French gun.

Next moment the French fired, their shell whistling harmlessly right across the top of the other bunker to explode in the fields beyond. He had rattled them!

The screech of the shell just above his head woke Major Kranz to his danger at last. He shook his head, as if he were waking up from a heavy sleep. Pushing aside the dead body of an infantryman who lay slumped across him, and wiping the man's blood from his face, he cried, 'Follow me!'

Not looking to see who was dead and who was alive in the pile of field-grey bodies, he ran groggily to the shell-hole the big gunner NCO had pointed out to him. With his pistol in one hand, he clambered over the debris, clawing aside the iron wires that had been used to pour the ferro-concrete. A little group of shaken, grey infantry crowded round him.

Again the French gun spoke. The shock-wave swept past them, slapping their clothes to their sweating bodies and leaving them breathless. But the shrapnel of the exploding shell whizzed by outside harmlessly. The French gun could no longer do them any harm. They were inside the fort.

Kranz dropped into the rubble-littered, gloomy corridor and crouched there, pistol in hand, while the infantry followed one by one. Kranz counted them by the sound of their boots hitting the concrete. There were exactly six of them, Six men to conquer a French fort, probably held by at least a company. He waited until the last man was inside, then he faced them. Voice sunk to a whisper, he said, 'Now listen, I haven't an idea in hell what the situation here is. All I know is that we're inside — and they don't know.' He bit his lip at the lie. How did *he* know? 'So we've got the advantage of surprise on our side. Clear?'

'Clear, Major,' the infantry whispered, but their eyes showed they were not altogether convinced.

'All right, follow me in single file. Three of you close to me — three bringing up the rear, last man covering our backs. Move out!'

Commandant Joubert whirled the handle of the field telephone furiously once more. 'Hello,' he barked into the speaker, the sweat dripping off his high forehead, 'can you read me there? Is there anyone there in the—'

The thump of the Boche shell against his bunker drowned his words and he raised his voice to bellow the rest of his information. 'Listen, half a dozen of the bastards have broken in from the roof. Do you read me now? Half a dozen of them have broken in!'

But no one in the bunker's control room read him. It was unoccupied save for Captain LeGrand's hideously mutilated body and a lone soldier, his trousers black with his own urine, who crouched in the corner, knees drawn to his face, hands pressed close to his ears, the tears streaming down his terrified young face unchecked.

Joubert let the phone fall back into its cradle. Now he knew there was no hope for the other bunker.

After the ear-splitting racket of the bombardment outside, the sudden silence was oppressive. Still Kranz pressed on down the long inky tunnel into the unknown. It seemed endless. Yet the Major reasoned that the fort's main installations would be in the centre, where they would receive the most protection from the concrete and earth walls.

The little band crept round a corner. Nothing. The place seemed abandoned. They stole on, feeling an increasing warmth on their grey faces. They must be close to the centre of this eerie place now. Suddenly Kranz stopped and held up his hand. He had heard a strange rattling sound. For a moment he could not locate it. Then he had it. It was coming from behind what looked like an iron door to his right. Swiftly he explained what he intended to do. The trained infantrymen nodded their understanding grimly. They all knew the dangers of this type of fighting. One slip and the element of surprise would be gone; they would be sitting ducks then.

They positioned themselves on either side of the metal door, which could be opened by a handle high up on the surface. Kranz waited till the soldier who was going to open it had a grip of the handle. He took a deep breath and yelled, *'NOW!'*

The soldier flung the door open. Yellow light streamed out. Kranz caught a glimpse of six French soldiers grouped round a machine gun, faces blackened with powder, floor littered with shining, smoking cartridges, and then he was in, firing from the hip. Once, twice, three times. His first two slugs missed. But the third one found a target. A bearded Frenchman went down screaming, his broad back blasted wide open at such short range.

'Levez les mains!' Kranz gasped in his awkward French, jerking his pistol upwards.

The gesture worked. The astonished gunners flung up their hands violently, as if they were carrying out some gymnastic exercise. For a moment Kranz swayed there wondering what to do with them. But then the look of absolute astonishment on the enemy's faces told him he could take advantage of this situation. *'Vous êtes le grand chef?'* he demanded of a burly, middle-aged man with medal ribbons and the golden stripes of an NCO on his sleeve.

'Non, non, Monsieur le Commandant,' the other man answered, and broke into a flood of heavily accented French, which Major Kranz could not understand.

Desperately Kranz cried, *'Fermez la bouche!'* He licked parched lips, trying to remember the French he had long forgotten. *'Où est le chef maintenant?'*

The middle-aged Sergeant-Major pointed upwards and Kranz understood that the CO of the fort was a lieutenant named Doux, who was somewhere in an observation tower. He made a quick decision. There was no telephone in the turret, so the French gunners could not contact the outside.

'Lock them in,' he commanded his infantry. 'You,' he waved his pistol at the Sergeant-Major. 'Take me to the Lieutenant.'

With the gunners imprisoned in their turret, the little group set off once more, this time with the French NCO leading the way, hands stretched straight up above his head as if his very life depended on keeping them as high as possible. In a way, it did.

Time passed leadenly. The corridors seemed endless. Kranz felt his nervousness grow by the moment, as their heavy boots echoed down the stone passages. Was the Frenchman leading them into a trap? He tightened his grip on the pistol with a hand that was wet with sweat.

Suddenly, another shell crashed into the fort, but this time so close that the roar was not muffled as up to now, but loud and frightening. It caught Kranz and his men off guard. So it was that in that same moment that the lights flickered and went out altogether, he did not react quickly enough as the French NCO broke loose and started running down the corridor. He pressed the trigger of his pistol. Scarlet flame stabbed the inky darkness. But the slug howled off the wall harmlessly and a moment later the running man had disappeared round a bend, leaving them crouched there helplessly in the black passage, hopelessly lost in the interior of the enemy-held fort.

'Well?' the General snapped, as he peered through his binoculars at the crumbling French fort. 'Are they still holding out? My schedule is four hours off, Captain, you know.' He lowered the glasses and looked accusingly at Captain Gehendges, as if he were personally responsible for the trouble the Maginot Line was causing.

An unshaven, bleary-eyed Gehendges, his pince-nez set crookedly on his nose, looked at the General helplessly. 'I don't know, sir,' he gulped.

To the rear, the other fort fired again. Obviously some keen-eyed French observation had seen the metal flag flying from the standard of the halftrack which Rommel had used to reach the most exposed part of his front. The halftrack disappeared for a moment and the elegant staff officers ducked over their messages and maps as the near miss showered them with mud and gravel.

'You don't know, Captain?' Rommel said icily. 'And what am I supposed to take that for – the work of some damned mole or other, eh? Answer me.'

'*Herr General,*' Schott, every inch the regular NCO, cut in, trying to save his wretched CO from the General's wrath.

'What is it, Sergeant-Major?' Rommel barked impatiently.

'There is a flag flying over the first bunker.'

'What? Let me see.' Rommel threw up his field glasses and focused them hastily with feverish fingers. '*Mei,*' he exclaimed, using the Swabian peasant expression, 'it's our flag! It's the swastika. They've done it . . . *they've done it!*'

Another slug howled into the debris of the observation tower. An infantryman yelped with pain and clapped his hand to his wounded shoulder, but his companion, holding the flag, still kept waving it furiously, as Kranz had ordered him to do.

Kranz, kneeling to the front, hidden by a block of fallen concrete, aimed and fired down the corridor at the French crouched there. Was his trick never going to work, he asked himself as yet another Frog slipped forward in spite of his slugs.

Now there were about a couple of dozen of them at the end of the corridor, led by an eager young officer who showed a complete disregard of his own safety, and they were moving forward with ever increasing boldness. Obviously the NCO who had slipped away had told them their attackers numbered only six and one officer. Another couple of *chasseurs* doubled forward. Both Kranz's pistol and the infantryman's rifle next to him fired instantly. A man fanned the air with crazy, dying fingers and flopped down with a slam onto the hard concrete, but two of his comrades had managed the rush successfully. Now they were only fifteen metres away from the men trapped at the end of the corridor.

'A couple more rushes like that, sir,' the infantryman

67

commented, expressing Kranz's own thoughts, 'and they'll have us by the knackers.'

'Shut up,' Kranz ordered. 'Concentrate on your front.' He raised his voice above the whine-and-snap of the small arms fire, 'And you waving the flag — wave the bastard, as if you were carrying the shitty banner at the Nürnberg Party Rally. *Wave!*'

Slowly Joubert lowered his binoculars. There was no mistaking it. The flag was the hated crooked cross of Nazi Germany. The Boche had taken LeGrand's bunker. For one long moment he stared blankly at the concrete wall a couple of millimetres away. What was he to do?

Honour had been satisfied. He knew that. The two bunkers had held out since dawn against what appeared to be a whole Boche division. But was that enough? He thought of his father, the 'Old General', as the servants called him back on the estate, blind and dumb, struck silent and sightless by a German shell, leading his division to the attack in 1918. What would he have done? Joubert did not know. His father had never once spoken to him since he had been a very small child.

Joubert licked his dry lips. Was anything worth that kind of fate? Could France expect that kind of loyalty, when its leaders were either crooks, filling their own pockets, cowards, scared of their own shadows, or collaborators who preferred the Germans to the English? In the final analysis, why should he sacrifice his young life for a country that had already betrayed the Army long before the war had started?

Joubert made his decision. He pressed the switch of the public address system. It came to life with a metallic hum. His voice completely unemotional, he commenced his message, not knowing that he, in his small way, was condemning *la belle France* to four years of treachery, degradation, and petty self-seeking. Four years from which she would not recover for another three decades. 'Soldiers, comrades, you have fought bravely. You have done enough. I will not demand the last sacrifice from you . . .'

Even before he had said the fateful last words, he could already hear the cheers of relief from below. 'No, comrades, I shall hand the fort over to the enemy . . . Break up your weapons, and . . .'

Joubert could not finish. He let his head slump against the wall, and down below the cheering men fell suddenly silent as the metallic, heartbroken sobs echoed down the abruptly still corridors.

'It's not possible!' the wounded soldier with the flag gasped.

'What—' Kranz ducked as the bullet howled off the wall just above his head — 'what is not possible?' he gasped.

'They're coming out.'

'The Frogs?'

'Yes,' the infantryman cried in delight, 'with their flippers above their heads. They're surrendering!'

A hoarse cheer rose from the weary little group of trapped infantrymen.

Kranz summoned up the last of his French. In a cracked voice, his mouth cupped in his hands, he called, '*Soldats, camarades, la guerre est fini pour vous. Écoutez moi, la guerre est fini.*' Gingerly he raised himself, half-expecting a French slug to whack into his fully exposed body at any moment and peered down the corridor, pistol hanging down in one hand in a gesture of peace. '*C'est tout fermé!* . . . *Comprenez — fini, tout fini.*' he added, his confidence growing with every fresh second. '*Les Allemands sont vos amis maintenant!*'

Taking his life into his hands, he thrust his pistol into its holster and began walking down the long corridor towards the French positions, his boots echoing down the stone passage. He had won.

General Erwin Rommel raised his binoculars. The second fort's great door to the rear had opened. Now the *poilus* streamed out into the May sunlight, blinking and dazed for a moment, then jabbering, pushing, screaming and cursing as they stumbled towards the German positions, waving makeshift flags. 'Why have you been so long?' they screamed when they saw the immaculate officer staring down at them from his half-track, shaking their fists at him. 'Why didn't you deliver us from our whoresons of officers earlier?'

Rommel lowered his binoculars slowly, ignoring them as they slipped and stumbled over the debris to the waiting cages to the rear. He was witnessing the breakdown of a nation, he knew it instinctively. The French had played the wrong cards for years; now they had lost the game for good. Slowly his tight lips moved a resolution. *And now for the Tommies . . .*

BOOK TWO: THE TOMMIES

ONE: ARRAS, 21st MAY, 1940

ONE

The skinny Irish general with the trim Regular British Army moustache stared out of the window of the Corps HQ in distaste. In the middle of the broken Belgian Army streaming past below, the soldiers bearing white flags on the end of their long World War One bayonets, a Belgian general had halted his staff car. In full sight of the broken, demoralized troops fleeing to the coast, the man stripped off his khaki uniform and changed into a sports coat and immaculately creased flannels before driving on again, horn honking, as if he were some rich tourist in a hurry to get to Deauville for the summer season.

The weary Belgian soldiers, retreating from the advancing Germans, filed on. They were followed by a group of lunatics, obviously escaped from some bombed asylum. Wearing the same brown corduroy suits, they struggled down the dusty road, grinning at the watching Tommies with inane smiles, saliva running from the corners of their slack mouths and dripping from their chins.

General Alan Brooke, the Corps Commander, turned away in disgust, telling himself that nothing but a miracle could save the British Expeditionary Force in France now. In view of what he had seen below, the Belgian Army must be regarded as completely broken. What the French were doing, he did not know. But he did know that after their successful retreat from Belgium, the British Army to which his Corps belonged were for it now.

There was a knock at the door. He cast aside his gloomy thoughts. 'Come,' he rapped.

The door opened to admit a brisk, birdlike figure clad in the new battledress which he affected while his fellow generals still wore the traditional service dress, complete with gleaming Sam Browne and sword sling. It was General Bernard Montgomery,

75

commander of the 3rd Division – 'the Iron Division', as they had called it in the First World War.

He extended his hand, a smile crossing his dark weary face. 'Monty, glad to see you. My message got through all right, I see?'

'Just,' his subordinate commander answered with a suspicion of a lisp. 'The refugees and the Hun fifth column are making a mess of the roads to the rear. The DR[1] took ages.'

Brooke nodded his understanding and said, 'Come on over here, Monty.'

'Yes, I'd like to have a look at the form, Brookie.' The skinny General with the beak of a nose walked over to the map which covered one wall of the office.

Brooke slapped the map in disgust. 'As you know, we are presently holding the line – still – here. But for how long I don't know. It's clear that those three Panzer divisions coming down from Sedan are heading straight for it. Now if they turn swiftly at Abbeville here and drive for the ports from Dunkirk to Boulogne – here – an entire French army, and our own chaps, would be cut off. We'd be split from our sea communications. Ammo is already very scarce, but if they got our ports, we'd run out of everything in, say, three days.'

'Well, Brookie, I didn't realize it was that serious. Haven't we got anything near the coast to stop them?'

'Not a thing.'

'What's the drill then? A counter-attack?'

'You've hit the nail on the head, Monty. Of course, not with infantry alone. They'd be slaughtered by those Boche tanks. We need tanks.'

'We could use the Corps' own infantry tanks. Our Mathildas are a match for anything the Jerry has.'

Brooke nodded his agreement. 'I'm planning to scrape together as many Mathildas I can lay my hands on and I want two battalions of infantry from you.'

'You have them.'

'Thanks,' Brooke said gratefully. Montgomery, who could be
[1] Despatch rider.

a very obstinate cuss, was backing him to the hilt. 'I also need anti-tank guns.'

'Well, the anti-tank rifle my infantry is issued with is useless against the Boche armour. Why don't you turn a battery of 25-pounder field guns into anti-tank artillery. They'll stop anything the enemy has.'

'Excellent idea, Monty,' Brooke said. 'Excellent.'

The two generals improvised a counter-stroke against the Panzers rushing west on a collision course, until finally the birdlike 3rd Division commander stopped. 'Where do we halt them, Brookie?'

'Here,' General Brooke slapped the map firmly. 'Here on the western environs of Arras, as soon as their lead division begins to hook northwards toward Lille.'

'Yes, that should be a good enough indication that they're heading for the sea in attempt to cut us off.'

'That is my opinion, too.'

Montgomery pointed to the marker on the map, already covered with a rash of blue lines, that indicated the leading German Panzer division heading west. 'I've forgotten my specs. Can't read the name, Brookie. What division is it, please?'

'The 7th Panzer. It's miles ahead of its running mate, the 5th Panzer — here.'

'Any idea who commands it, Brookie?'

'Rommel, a General Erwin Rommel.' Brooke mentioned the name that Montgomery would come to respect and hate in the years to come, for the first time.

'Never heard of him,' the little General barked firmly and glared at the long blue line on the map. 'But all I can say is that the chap is so far out that he's going to get a very bloody nose if he doesn't watch out.'

Brooke looked across at his subordinate, the worry clear in his dark eyes behind the thick, horn-rimmed spectacles. 'Let's hope so, Monty. Because if we don't stop him this time, we and the rest of the BEF will be running for the sea.'

'Never fear, Brookie,' Montgomery said with characteristic confidence. 'This Rommel fellow will get his bloody nose.'

Thus he left, stalking out into the confused mess of the farmyard HQ, ready to do battle for the first time with a man against whom he would fight half a hundred battles.

TWO

Now the 25th Panzer Regiment rolled on, kilometres ahead of the rifle regiments. Everywhere the countryside was draped in white. From every red-brick tumbledown house, farm, church steeple, school, a white sheet, a table-cloth, a towel — even a handkerchief — served as a white flag. The whole of Northern France seemed to have surrendered.

Most of the villages, through which the victorious tanks rolled, were heavily shuttered and empty, though the tankers, sleeves rolled up and faces glowing in the May heat, sensed anxious ears were being pressed to the wood trying to make out every sound the invader made. But here and there there were little knots of silent civilians who watched the might of Nazi Germany swing past, some of them crying, some openly hostile, but with most of them looking at their conquerors in numb resignation.

Still, Colonel Rothenburg was taking no chances, in spite of General Rommel's impatient order: '*Advance to the sea — and damn your flanks!*' The country was now ideal for an ambush. It was flat, stretching in dreary marshy greenness as far as the eye could see, and devoid of trees save those which lined the dead-straight roads. But it was crisscrossed by canals and roads at right angles to each other, which would make an excellent offensive line; and as each field was below the level of its particular canal, it also had its own diminutive dike running around it: an excellent place to conceal infantry, or even tanks. But as the hot morning wore on and the only enemy the 25th Panzer encountered was fleeing, ragged and dirty *poilus*, who had long thrown away their weapons and raised their arms in surrender immediately the first German tanks appeared, Colonel Rothenburg became careless.

The thought of the Knight's Cross of the Iron Cross, which he would undoubtedly receive from the *Führer* for being the first commander to reach the sea, spurred him on to take risks which he would not normally have taken. The 25th Panzer clattered through the featureless countryside, past canals choked with wrecked and abandoned French and British vehicles, heading straight into the trap.

'Here they come,' Captain Smithers whispered, and wiped the sweat from his dripping palms on the back of his battledress trousers. 'Ready, one, two and three?'

The three bombardiers wearing the red-and-black triangle of the 'Iron Division' rapped back their answers, while to their front the gun-layers followed the progress of the squat monsters, silhouetted black against the red sun, as they rolled along the elevated road three hundred yards away.

Smithers swallowed hard and picked up his Very pistol. It was a gunner's dream, but after ten years in the Territorials and nine months on active service, this would be his first action. He knew that in one moment he would be committing himself and his men to an irrevocable course. There would be no going back. He cocked the pistol and raised it above his head.

With startling finality the flare hissed into the burning hot sky. For what seemed a very long time it hung there, spurting out a shower of silver sparks into the bright red before it fell, sweeping down like a fallen angel.

There was nothing angelic about the next moment. The earth shook. Red lights rippled along the line of the dikes, as the other 25-pounder batteries saw the signal. White, burning armour-piercing shells hurtled towards the surprised Panzers, increasing in speed at every moment. The battle had commenced. The enemy had been caught by complete surprise.

'Anti-tank fire,' Colonel Rothenburg screamed in alarm. 'Deploy—'

The rest of his sentence was drowned by the thunderous clash of metal against metal. His Mark III skidded over the side of the road and shot into the ditch, thick, white, choking smoke pouring from its shattered engine.

Behind him the tank of his second-in-command shuddered as if it had just run into a brick wall. Its left track flipped off like a suddenly severed limb. It, too, came to a dead halt. In an instant the point of the victorious 25th Panzer Regiment was a blazing metal chaos, with the afternoon air full of the acrid stink of burning cordite, scorched metal and charred human flesh. The way forward was blocked.

'Holy strawstack,' von Fromm cursed, 'they've gone and caught us with our knickers down!'

'Shut up,' Kranz's voice crackled over the ether. 'Cover us at point.' His command tank shuddered violently in the wake of a 25-pound shell which had just missed the turret. 'I want to see if we can get out of this shitting mess.'

'Will do,' von Fromm called cheerfully. 'Nothing must stop the Guard, what. Out and over!'

His handsome young face set in a sudden look of determination, monocle firmly screwed in his eye, he commanded, 'Gunner – traverse left . . . Tommy 25-pounder two o'clock . . . *Fire!*'

Hurriedly, von Fromm's gunner swung his 75mm round to take up the British challenge, his fingers twirling round the elevator wheel rapidly.

The air in front of the Mark IV flashed a brilliant, blinding yellow. The turret rocked like a rattled toy. Blast filled the open turret and von Fromm opened his mouth instinctively to prevent his eardrums from bursting, just as the steaming yellow shell case rattled to the metal floor. He peered hurriedly through the periscope.

'Short, you blind bastard!' he yelled. 'Up one hundred!'

Frantically the gunner shoved home another round in to the gaping breech. Automatically the breech-lever clicked up. The breech was closed. Crazily the gunner upped his range. Von Fromm waited an instant. 'Now,' he commanded. 'Fire!'

The 20-ton tank shuddered once more. Again the blast slapped them in the faces and made them close their eyes. Von Fromm peered through the periscope. The cloud of smoke cleared. Where the 25-pounder had been, there was a steaming hole littered with bits and pieces of men and metal. A headless body of what had once been the gun-commander hung from a nearby tree, swinging back and forth with the blast.

To his rear another couple of guns opened up. The second tank of the 404th's point disappeared in a ball of red flame. Von Fromm felt the frightening whiplash as the second shell whooshed by his own tank.

Von Fromm pressed the throat mike. 'Driver, get the hell off this road! We're a sitting duck up here. At the double!'

The driver fumbled his gears in his panic. The tank lurched forward, instead of backwards, dropping straight over the embankment directly exposed to the British fire.

'Oh, my aching ass!' von Fromm cursed. 'You son of a five-mark whore. Now you've really gone and done it!'

Behind him on the road the last of the three tanks at point exploded in flame, its commander's overall a mass of angry flame as he ran screaming wildly down the road after the departing squadron until he dropped, a charred, disfigured heap.

Von Fromm made a quick decision, now that he was all alone. 'Up the guard!' he yelled with crazed exuberance. 'Let's charge the buck-toothed buggers!'

The Mark IV rolled over the flat marshy countryside. A vicious burst of white tracer hissed at it from the flank. Von Fromm heard it rattle harmlessly along the turret. He swung the m.g. round. A two-man Bren crew, easily recognizable in the pudding-basin English helmets, were trying to flee to the cover of the nearest canal. Von Fromm pressed the trigger. The weapon sprang to life in his hand. At 800 rounds per minute it cut the two men down in the first burst. Next moment the tank had rolled over their writhing bodies, squashing them to pulp in the mud.

'Tommy gun, ten o'clock!' the driver screamed frantically in a paroxysm of terror.

Von Fromm spun the turret round. Hidden by two poplars, a British 25-pounder was turning its stubby barrel in their direction. Von Fromm's gunner beat the Tommies to it. He ripped back the firing bar. The AP shell ripped into the 25-pounder's shield. Metal and men flew through the air and the shell the Tommies had fired in that very same instant hissed by harmlessly.

The Mark IV lurched violently. The turret was filled with a searing heat. Von Fromm stared horrified at the inner wall. It had suddenly turned a glowing red. He knew immediately what had happened. An AP shell had hit the thick metal and was now working its way — by some trick of ballistics — around it. Eyes wide with terror he watched the red glow spread. In one minute they could all be blown to hell. And then as suddenly as it had appeared, the glow had vanished and the shell was howling off into space.

'Whew!' he gasped and wiped the dripping sweat from his purple face. 'That was close.' With an effort, he pulled himself together, all ambition to earn a decoration for bravery on this particular occasion disappeared. The odds were too great even for a von Fromm.

'Driver, don't shit me about anymore. We're getting out of here — and quick. See that clump of trees at four o'clock. Head for it — and leave the rest to me.'

As the driver swung the tank round, von Fromm raised himself above the turret, ignoring the concentrated tracer fire which directed itself on him immediately. To his right the mass British batteries were still pounding the hopelessly trapped 25th Panzer Regiment's point. To his left Major Kranz was nowhere to be seen. He had managed apparently to break off the action successfully. He could safely retire, his honour unimpaired.

As he had half-expected, the anti-tank gun concealed in the clump of poplars opened up on him immediately. But von Fromm had one last trick up his sleeve. When the gunners of the 25-pounder were firing at him over open sights and he could see their frantic crimson faces quite clearly, he pulled the two smoke dischargers. Thick white smoke blinded them immediately. 'Don't hesitate,' von Fromm yelled wildly. 'Nothing can stop the Guard!'

There was the hollow booming sound of metal striking metal. The Mark IV came to an abrupt halt as it rammed the 25-pounder. Von Fromm did not hesitate. 'Abandon tank!' he ordered and, freeing himself from the radio wires, dropped over the side, pistol barking as he did so. But it was unnecessary. The British crew lay sprawled around their gun in the extravagant postures of those who have died violently.

Von Fromm waited till the driver had crawled out from the emergency hatch and then the three of them were pelting crazily over the wet fields, leaving the burning ruins of what was left of Colonel Rothenburg's column behind them.

The triumphant dash of the 7th Panzer Division for the sea had come to an abrupt and bloody halt.

THREE

It was like a furnace. The oblique glare of the late May sun across the French fields cut into the eyes like a knife. Above, the sky was smoke-coloured and ominous. Through it the sun glittered like a copper coin. The heat rippled in blue waves across the high grass. It seemed as if the heat of the battle had communicated itself to nature; as if the whole countryside was ablaze.

Wearily, Major Kranz thrust his beret to the back of his head and waited until the General's halftrack had drawn up beside him in the swirling dust. Along the road, Colonel von Bismarck's infantry trucks rolled in a slow solid line that stretched back kilometres, heading ever westwards, the crimson-faced soldiers, heads bound in handkerchiefs, fast asleep with utter exhaustion.

'Well?' Rommel demanded, and for once there was an anxious look on his foxlike face. 'What is the situation like up front?'

'Shitty,' Kranz said, angry at the losses his own command had suffered. 'Decidedly shitty, *Herr General.*'

'And what is that supposed to mean?'

'Exactly what I say, sir,' Kranz snapped, unable to pull his punches; after all, he had lost four tanks of the remaining 14, including von Fromm's. And he knew why. Rommel had pushed his armoured point out too far without the cover of infantry. Bitterly he explained in a few harsh words what had happened to Colonel Rothenburg's 25th Panzer Regiment.

'What?' Rommel exclaimed when he was finished. 'Do you mean to say there is nothing between my two rifle regiments,' he indicated the long grey line of trucks edging by, 'and the enemy?'

'It looks exactly like that, sir,' Kranz answered, not attempting to spare the General. 'The Tommies caught us completely by surprise. It wasn't just chance. They had been waiting for us from well-prepared positions — and they gave us hell. In my company I lost . . .' He stopped short, when he realized that Rommel was not listening. Instead he licked his cracked, parched lips and told himself he would give a small fortune at this moment for an ice-cold glass of beer.

Rommel made some quick decisions. Without turning round, he snapped at Schraepler, his aide, 'Captain, get on to Air. I need Stukas. Stukas *at once*! And tell those fly-boys that if I don't get them, I'll report the matter personally to the *Führer*.' He looked up at the weary Kranz. 'You, Major, I want you to head for the rear – hell-for-leather – and bring up that flak captain with the pince-nez. What the devil is his name?' He clicked his fingers impatiently.

'Gehendges, Captain Gehendges,' Kranz volunteered.

'That's right. Tried to talk me into buying some insurance last night. The nerve. Anyway, get him up with the rifle regiment, immediately.'

'May I ask why, sir?'

'Well, isn't it obvious?' Rommel shrilled, his raw nerves showing through for an instant. 'The Tommies have cut us off from our armour, they're after the fat pickings – the infantry. And those pea-shooters out there,' he indicated the screen of 37mm anti-tank guns bumping along to their right on the secondary road, 'won't be able to ward them off. Now get on with it, or we're going to be in serious trouble.'

'More!' Captain Gehendges commanded with more authority than he had ever felt in all his life, *'plus – comprenez? – Plus!'* He puffed at the big cigar and took another sip of the excellent scotch, both looted from a British dump.

'Oui, oui, mon General,' the little French prisoner they had picked up along the way said eagerly and doubled away to fetch some more hot water for the tub.

Gehendges leaned back in the big wooden tub set in the middle of the boiling hot field and told himself that things were going well after all. The war had passed him by and soon there would be peace, perhaps even a few half-naked whores in sheer black silk stockings.

86

All around him, his men lay half-naked in the sun, letting its healing warmth burn into their tired bones and kill the lice with which they were all infected. Someone was playing a mouth organ and singing softly— the usual evocative blend of 'homeland' and 'loved ones' — while Sergeant-Major Schott, his wounded arm strapped firmly to his side, was counting out the wads of French francs he had 'organized' that morning, in between taking mighty swigs of his 'medicine', a fifty-litre carboy of cognac.

'Peace, perfect peace,' Gehendges sighed and blew a contented stream of rich blue smoke at the flies which buzzed at the edge of the tub of hot water, scented with a whole bottle of expensive cologne, also supplied by the ever resourceful Sergeant-Major Schott. 'Now this is what I really call war.' He closed his eyes and settled back luxuriously, his mind full of black silk and shapely legs.

'Gehendges!' The voice was harsh and urgent.

He flicked open his short-sighted eyes and groaned. He closed them again, as if he hoped he might blot out what he saw there. To no avail. Kranz was very much there. 'Is there anything the matter?' he tried hopefully.

'And how!' Kranz barked. 'The Tommies are threatening to cut the Division in half at any moment. They've blocked us with anti-tank guns, so the General thinks they might attack with tanks right into the infantry. That's why you are to come with me. He needs anti-tank guns.'

'But we're flak,' Gehendges protested, realizing as he said the words that he had said them before to no purpose.

'Yes, I know all that. Now will you get your fat arse out of that bath and move. Time is running out and the General has promised us both a medal if we can stop the Tommies.'

Mentally Gehendges told the weary, dirty Major what to do with his medal. But he heaved himself, dripping with suds, from the bath like an overgrown whale and called: 'Sergeant-Major . . . Sergeant-Major Schott. I need you here immediately.' It was the cry of a selfish child for its mother . . .

FOUR

A pall of smoke, mingled with the growing darkness, lay over the impending battlefield. But the shivering, nervous gunners of the light 37mm anti-tank guns, which screened the Ghost Division, could hear the rumble of heavy tanks somewhere to their right and knew that the coming battle was not far off. Softly, as if not wishing to startle the edgy anti-tank gunners, their officers went from position to position, checking that every gun was ready, and calming their men with the usual lies that officers tell their men on such occasions. 'Tremendous reserves are hurrying up to support us . . . the General himself is on the way . . . Never fear, their tanks are made of pressed cardboard . . .'

But the weary, hollow-eyed young gunners knew the truth. There was not a hope in hell of their 37mm shell penetrating the armour of the British infantry tanks.

Now the earth started to shudder. All along the German line, the star shells hissed into the darkness. Officers yelled orders, NCOs blew their shrill whistles. And the gunners tensed behind their little cannon. In the harsh, cruel light of the star shells, rank after rank of heavy tanks emerged from the dip to their front. The CO of the anti-tank screen started to count them with lips that were suddenly dry. *Twenty . . . thirty . . . forty . . . fifty . . .* Helplessly he gave up counting, knowing that his fate and that of his men was already sealed. The General had condemned them to death in this exposed position with their absurd pop-guns.

Behind their guns, the young soldiers held their breath and watched, as if mesmerized, while the iron wave of death swept ever closer, rolling in with the power and majesty of nature itself. Then the strange, somnabulant advance halted. The gunners knew why. The Tommies were preparing to fire. But their own limbs were strangely numb. They still could not move.

Like the roar of an infuriated beast trapped in a cage, the tanks opened up. Countless flashes of scarlet cut the gloom. Golden-white tracer hissed across the intervening distance. At last the anti-tank gunners awoke from their trance. Frantically they spun their guns round, eyes pressed to the rubber suction-pads of the sights, hands whirling the brass wheels crazily. And then the bombardment submerged them.

Gun after gun rose into the air in absurd slow-motion, taking with it the gory bits and pieces of flesh that had once been men. Men buried their heads in their hands, unable to take that terrible fire. Officers screamed at them hysterically. But to no avail. Their own shells were bouncing off the Mathildas like ping-pong balls. And now the Tommies were advancing again. It would be a matter of minutes before they overran the anti-tank screen completely.

Watching the one-sided battle by the blaze of fire and counter-fire, Major Kranz bit his lip. It would take another hour before Gehendges with his slower gun-towing vehicles would be in position on the high ground to his rear, and although he knew Rommel had ordered up the Stukas, there was still no sign of the fly-boys. What was he to do?

And then the Stukas came sweeping in like sinister black hawks. Kranz breathed out a sigh of relief. Behind, what was left of his tankers burst into loud cheers. 'Go on, lovely boys, get the Tommy bastards!' someone yelled enthusiastically.

The first flight peeled off. Sirens screaming hideously, they seemed to fall out of the sky, dropping like stones, as if they were heading straight for the earth. When it seemed they would never be able to pull out of the dive again, the leader rose, a myriad black eggs tumbling out of its blue-painted belly. One after another, his flight did the same, and the stick of bombs exploded directly in the German positions.

'Oh, my God!' Kranz choked. 'They've hit our boys!' In the darkness and confusion, the Stuka pilots had obviously not recognized the swastika identification panels which the gunners had spread out in front of their positions.

'Radioman,' he bellowed, 'get onto HQ. Tell them the flyboys are bombing—'

But it was already too late. The next flight had already peeled off. Zooming down at 300 kilometres an hour, sirens screaming, wind brakes down so that they looked like buzzards coming in for the kill, the second flight, too, dropped its deadly cargo directly on the anti-tank positions.

And then as abruptly as they had appeared, the Stukas flew off to East again, undoubtedly, as Kranz told himself bitterly, to celebrate their 'victory' with looted French champagne and eager local whores. But there was no time for recriminations. The Tommies were advancing again and what were left of the dazed, bloody gunners were preparing to make their last defence before they were completely overwhelmed by the Mathildas.

Kranz made his decision. He pressed his mike button. 'Attention all crew commanders. I'm going on alone. Yes, *alone*!' he repeated, as if he expected some protest. 'You are to remain here and defend this position until the 88s appear. Remember, you must hold on till they come up. Good luck – and thanks to you all.' He controlled the sudden sob in his voice with difficulty. 'Over and out.'

'Driver – *advance*!' Slowly the lone tank began to rumble down the incline to meet the armoured might of the British Army. Sadly the crews watched their CO disappear into the growing gloom, telling themselves they would never see Major Kranz again. He was surely going to his death.

'Driver – *halt*!' Kranz commanded, his voice seeming to belong to someone else.

Ahead of him there were only a handful of 37mms still firing. Their line had been virtually swamped by the Mathildas, which were swirling back and forth over the gunpits, crushing to death the screaming men who crouched there.

'Gunner – traverse left – ten o'clock. British Mathilda – range six five zero.' He forced himself to give the order with pre-war training-ground precision, knowing as he did so he was virtually condemning himself to death. What could a lone tank do against the massed British armour?

He watched as his new gunner, Schmidt, turned the range-drum to the correct range and then pressed his eye to the telescope, his face hollowed out to a death's head in the eerie dim green light. *'Fire!'* he barked.

The Mark IV rocked slightly. Smoke and flame spurted up in front of his eyes. For an instant he could follow the solid armour-piercing shot as it curved upwards in slow motion before it hurtled at tremendous speed towards its target. A soft boom, the unmistakeable dull-red glow of steel striking steel.

'Hit!' he cried enthusiastically, 'Schmidt, you old arsehole, you've got a hit!'

Ahead, one of the many Mathildas was beginning to burn furiously.

'Driver — advance. *For Chrissake, advance!*' he yelled, forgetting the first kill. For already raw jabs of angry flame were beginning to stab the gloom in his direction. Just in time. As the Mark IV lurched forward, a large oak just to its right fell with a great rending sound, sending earth flying high in the air and almost submerging the tank in its green gloom.

'Mathilda, five zero — eleven o'clock!' Kranz ordered, picking out the Tommy tank closest to him.

Schmidt whirled his wheels. 'On!' he bellowed.

'Fire!'

Again the Mark IV shuddered violently and Kranz caught a glimpse of the white tracer shell zipping flatly towards its target. The Mathilda rocked as if on a rough sea. Ugly red sparks flew up from its rear sprocket. At once furious white smoke started to stream from its engine cowling. In an instant it was a blazing torch, with its crew flinging themselves on the grass, trying to extinguish the flames which rose higher and higher and would not be extinguished.

'You did it—'

With a blow like a giant smith's hammer on an anvil, the first shell struck the Mark IV. Kranz was flung against the side

91

of the turret and felt his mouth fill with the salty taste of blood. In a flash all was chaos. Another shell hit the turret. A shock-wave hissed through the holed cupolas, singeing Kranz's face and leaving him breathless and bewildered. For a moment he could not move. He blinked several times, and finally his eyes focused. The turret was a shambles. Schmidt's head had vanished but his body was pinned upright by a stanchion which had transfixed him. Kranz fought back the vomit which threatened to choke him.

At his feet there were a myriad small tongues of purple flame, which licked greedily at the ammunition racks. 'Driver,' he ordered, mouth full of bitter bile, 'reverse!'

Nothing happened.

For what seemed an eternity, he could not work out why. Then he saw the reason. The radio had been melted into a shapeless mess by the AP shell. Fighting back his repulsion, he leaned over the headless body of the gunner and peered into the green gloom of the driver compartment below. 'Horst,' he croaked.

The driver's blackened face looked up at·him, the eyes seeming to be unnaturally white and terrified against the sudden black background. 'Sir?'

'*Reverse!*'

'I can't –' The Mark IV rocked violently again as another shell slammed into its side. There was the frightening stink of burning in the air now. To their front the stubby 75mm slumped down like a broken limb. Their gun was knocked out.

'For God's sake, let's get out of here. We've had it!' the driver cried in panic. 'The whole shitting Tommy army is firing on us—' Again his words were cut short by a solid thud of steel against their side.

'Bale out!' Kranz made his decision. '*Bale out at once, Horst!*' In a franzy of panic, the two survivors pulled themselves out of the emergency hatch, knowing that the Tommies would continue firing at the crippled German tank until they saw the flames, which would indicate their victim was well and truly killed.

The earth trembled. Kranz knew why. The Tommy armour was advancing once more. The anti-tank screen had been completely overrun and his own sacrifice had been for nothing. His throat feeling like sandpaper, he whispered, 'Come on Horst, let's get out of here. Their infantry will be coming mopping up in a minute.'

'Christ, I'd give a month's pay for a nice cool beer now,' Horst croaked and rose to his feet. 'You know, sir, my throat's like the bottom of a parrot's cage — full of dried shit.'

'You can talk,' Kranz said sourly, 'Come on.'

The minutes crawled. Everywhere there were English voices, excited and triumphant. Their infantry had obviously been just behind the tanks. The two of them pushed on, guided by the shouts on all sides. The English were looting the German positions. Kranz was filled with a sense of futility and inevitability of death. Was this — bayonetted to death by some unseen enemy on an obscure, nameless French field — what his life had been all about? Had all the anguish and joy, the happy childhood and the years of study, the flirtations, the love affairs and all the rest of it, been a simple preparation for a couple of moments of terror and pain before the light went out for ever?

'Sir,' Horst's frightened voice cut into his gloomy reverie.

'What is it?' he whispered.

'There's one of the bastards up ahead of us. Look.'

Kranz peered through the gloom. For a moment he could see nothing. Then he could just make out the silhouette of a man — and behind him yet another one — crouched there, motionless. He swallowed hard and reached for his pistol, telling himself he would sell himself dearly. The Tommies were not going to stick him like some dumb pig at the end of their long old-fashioned bayonets. He raised his pistol, whispering to his companion, 'Horst, you take the fellow on the right, I'll take the one on the left. Fire together on command — then run like hell.'

He took careful aim, listening to the shouts behind him

93

getting ever closer. Time was running out. His finger squeezed the trigger. It was now or never.

Suddenly he dropped the pistol and said sharply, 'Horst – *no*!'

'What is it, sir?'

He did not reply. Instead, he sniffed the air like a bloodhound scenting a trail. He knew that smell – the dry odour of an expensive perfume. It could only be—

Kranz burst forward. The next instant he was slapping the dirty-faced officer with a cracked monocle clamped in his eye furiously on the shoulder like a long-lost brother. He had found von Fromm and what was left of his crew!

'And now?' von Fromm asked, as the shivering men crouched in the cover of a thicket watching the Tommy tanks below forming up in the scarlet light of the burning German guns and transport. 'What is the position now?'

'Shitty,' Kranz said. 'Decidedly shitty. I've put you in the picture. What do you think?'

'The same,' von Fromm agreed with no trace of his affectation now, his monocle a crazy gleaming spider-web in the ruddy reflection of the flames. 'I suppose it's every man for himself?'

'Exactly. I don't think our fat insurance man's going to be able to stop those tanks down there. Do you?'

Von Fromm shook his head.

Wearily, Kranz rose to his feet. 'Come on, you lot,' he commanded, 'we'd better be on our way. The Ghost Division's had it . . .'

They staggered off eastwards into the darkness.

Rommel ducked instinctively and routinely. The stray enemy shell whizzed by and exploded with an asthmatic thump to the rear. He pressed the earphones closer to his shaven head and repeated his question: 'What did you say about the air strike.'

The faint crackling voice said, 'Totally failed. Hit our own troops.'

Rommel gritted his teeth. 'And the anti-tank screen?' he asked, as if he could not get enough of the bed news.

'Swept away, sir,' came the answer, crackling over air waves, which were heavy with static and excited voices jabbering away in three languages. 'Massive British tank attack — simply overrran them.'

Rommel absorbed the information, while to his front what was left of the 25th Panzer Regiment battled with the British, bogged down completely so that there was no way that they could break off the action and go to the aid of the threatened rifle regiments. 'What have we got left?' he asked finally.

'A thin screen of the 404th and the flak of the 6th.'

'They are in position?' he rapped quickly.

'Yes, on Height 222,' Colonel von Bismarck gave the code coordinate of the ridge. 'But there are only six of them left, and according to reports from the 404th, there must be at least sixty enemy tanks presently advancing on them. Besides, who really knows whether the 88mm can be used in the ground role?'

Rommel did not overlook the note of reproach in the infantry officer's voice. 'Now is the time to find out, Colonel,' he snapped. 'But that is not the point. They've got to stop the Tommies, even if they do it with their bare hands and boots. In the meantime halt and dig in.'

'Sir!'

'And if you are in radio contact with Captain Gehendges, tell him I shall break out here and come to give him my personal

95

support. That should do the trick, I shouldn't be surprised, eh, Colonel,' Rommel added.

'Yessir. I will do that,' von Bismarck answered dutifully, though as he signed off he told himself it would take Jesus Christ personally to save Captain Gehendges and his handful of gunners now.

Below, in the flat Flemish countryside, death and destruction stretched over the wet fields, still shrouded in wisps of grey fog that twirled and swirled around the shattered guns and wrecked trucks. Gehendges focused his glasses and surveyed the desolate scene. Here and there Tommies in their pudding-basin helmets crouched over fires made of ammunition crates, heating their morning tea probably, oblivious to the dead bodies in field-grey sprawled everywhere. But of the tanks who must soon attack Height 222, he could see nothing. The mist to the rear still concealed them.

He lowered the glasses and turned to an unshaven, grey-faced Schott, who had deep bags under his eyes due to exhaustion and lack of sleep.

'What do you think, Sergeant-Major?'

'I 'aint paid to think, Captain,' Schott growled grumpily. 'That's what we pay oficers and gents for.'

'Please, Sergeant-Major,' Gehendges pleaded.

Schott took his eyes off a truck driver, his guts ripped open so that the viscera swelled out of the gaping hole like a gigantic blood-red anemone. 'Well, seeing you ask me, I'll tell you, Captain,' he said grimly. 'This is what the Tommies are doing at this moment. They're forming up on both sides of this here height. They know they can't outflank us. It would be too dangerous. So they'll launch a two-pronged attack, probably with infantry, in the hope that we can't manage both flanks at once. It's simple. I read it in a book once.'

Gehendges wrung his pudgy, dirty hands. 'Oh my God, what are we going to do, Sergeant-Major?'

Schott took his time. He bit the dirt from underneath a nail and spat it out before looking at the other hand and deciding it would be too painful to repeat the procedure with it; then he said. 'Do? Easy Captain, we're gonna die, and hope we make handsome corpses.'

'Don't say that, *please* don't say things like that, even as a joke,' Gehendges quavered.

'No joke, Captain, it's the truth.'

'But we must be able to do something,' Gehendges persisted.

'Yer,' Schott said cruelly, '*pray*.' The big Sergeant-Major stalked off towards the gunners grouped around their cannon. The whole damned attack had been doomed to failure right from the very start. Rommel was typical of the 'New German', as the Nazis called themselves proudly, with their sickening, brown-uniformed, overweening confidence. He knew no boundaries. Everything and anything was possible in the 'New Germany', as if by being elected in 1933, Hitler had created a different race of men in half a dozen years, who did not need to live by the rules of ordinary mortals. And where had it got him and the rest of the brown pack? Right in the shit, up to their fat stupid faces. But they wouldn't have to suffer, pay for their mistakes with their lives. No, it would be the men around him who would go hop: little men, victims on the sacrificial altar of the 'New Order'.

Suddenly Sergeant-Major Schott was overwhelmed by a great rage. Dammit, he asked himself in anger, why should they die? By God, they wouldn't die, if he could help it.

He turned and stalked back to a pale-faced, ashen Gehendges. 'Listen, Captain,' he said gruffly, 'I watched those Tommy tankers just before they packed up for the night yesterday.'

Gehendges looked up at him numbly. His eyes were blank. He had already given up.

'And I noticed this. Their squadron commanders use flags to communicate with their tanks just like we did back in '37 before General Guderian[1] introduced a really effective radio communication system.'

Still Gehendges's face showered no interest.

'Now, that means they are vulnerable, very vulnerable. Knock

[1] The father of the German Panzer division.

out a squadron leader like that one with the flags, and you upset a whole squadron. Everyone knows the Tommies are sheep. They can't act independently. Something to do with six hundred years of democracy, I shouldn't be surprised. Now if we could do that, we'd certainly be able to —'

'Say that again, Sergeant-Major,' Gehendges interrupted him, with something like hope in his dull eyes.

Schott repeated his words.

'Do you mean that if we managed to kill the chaps with the flags, we'd be able to ward them off?'

'Perhaps not for good. But it'd certainly make them slow down. And by that time, the rest of the Division might have caught up with us. It's at least a chance.'

'Of course, of course, my dear Schott. What would I do without you, old chap?'

'What indeed,' Schott said sourly. 'Now then, I want the six best shots in the battery and I want them on the double. Can't you hear?'

Gehendges cocked his ear to one side. He went a pale yellow. There was no mistaking that sound. Many, many engines had suddenly started up below the cover of the mist. The Tommies were coming!

'All my life, I've believed that France has been cursed by a run of bad luck,' the weary French officer said in fluent German, while von Fromm and Kranz covered him with their pistols, and the rest of the survivors worked feverishly to get the staff car they had just shot up working again.

'Even as a kid the headlines in the papers always seemed to be the same — bad! Finance scandal. Government about to fall. Treasury bankrupt. Defeat for French diplomacy. Later, as a young man at the Sorbonne I remember seeing two mobs of different persuasions even yelling the *Marseillais* at each other. The hymn of our country was not even proof against bad luck.' He mopped his brow. 'In a way I'm glad it has ended like this. We've reached the nadir of our bad luck. Perhaps things will change—'

Suddenly the motor burst into life once more and drowned his words. Horst raised himself and said proudly, 'The sewing machine has started, *sir*.'

'Good work, Horst,' Kranz said and lowered his pistol.

The French officer looked at von Fromm, who still had his weapon levelled at him, a little apprehensively. 'Has my luck run out, too?' he asked, just a slight trace of fear in his young voice.

Von Fromm grinned from behind his cracked monocle. 'Only in a way, old friend.'

'What way?'

'Well, from now on, you're walking, and we're riding.' He thrust his pistol back in its holster and swung himself aboard after the rest in the same moment that the guns started to thunder somewhere to their right in the mist.

Kranz looked at von Fromm significantly. 'Gehendges,' he said.

'Well?'

'There's only one way to save him, von Fromm, and we're going to do it, whether General Erwin Johannes bloody Rommel likes it or not. We're going to bring up the 5th Panzer Division. Hit the gas, Horst!'

Horst hit the gas and the staff car shot away, leaving the French officer still squatting in the dust, bewailing his country's luck — but grateful for his own.

It was an awesome spectacle — twin streams of black-painted monsters waddling to left and right of the Height like ants on the march, unseeing, unfeeling, unable to be deflected from their grim purpose. Gehendges swallowed hard and prayed that Schott was right. He looked to left and right at his gunners. White-faced and tense, they were ready. He brought down his hand and yelled, *'Fire!'*

Cannon after cannon roared. A semi-circle of blinding light ran round their positions. A wild tearing noise struck the air. A Mathilda rocked violently and disappeared in a whirling mass of debris.

Time and time again, steel smashed into steel. Mathilda after Mathilda came to a halt, young troopers staggering out of their wrecked vehicles, white-faced and shocked. For years they had been told there was not an anti-tank gun in the world which would penetrate the armour of the Mathilda Mark II. Now this!

But still the metal wave crept forward, encircling the handful of guns on the height, threatening to swamp them soon. Schott gritted his teeth against the pain in his shoulder and tucked the rifle almost tenderly to his right cheek. He breathed out carefully and began to squeeze the trigger. What had the musketry instructor always said, though in another age? 'Squeeze it, as if you were squeezing your girlfriend's tits.' The butt of the rifle kicked against his shoulder, and there was a spurt of flame. As he rapidly ejected the spent cartridge, ready to fire again, he saw the Tommy tank officer with the enormous black moustache, like that of some 18th-century hussar, drop his little flags and flop down over his turret.

But still the Tommies came on.

Now their stubby cannon were opening up. Shells started to whizz over the heads of the hidden snipers and burst further up among the gunners. A lucky shell smashed into the barrel of the

88mm next to Gehendges. It split like a banana being peeled. The crew went reeling back, faces lacerated by metal splinters. Next instant the shell in its barrel exploded, zig-zagging crazily upwards.

Gehendges gasped with shock. 'My God,' he screamed at the burning heavens, 'how long can this go on!'

Down below Schott took aim again grimly. The Tommies were only two hundred metres away. It would not be long now before they were overrun. Suddenly his mind was overwhelmed by the horrifying vision of tank tracks turning and turning over his prostrate body, pulping and churning his unresisting flesh into a bloody gore. Hastily he pressed the trigger. Another Tommy commander flopped down dead. But still the Mathildas came on . . .

The haughty aristocratic commander of the 5th Panzer Division looked down his long nose at the two ragged, filthy officers standing rigidly to attention before his command halftrack. There was one with too long blond hair and — of all things — a cracked monocle in his eye. The other was obviously a civilian in uniform, in spite of his major's stars. 'Ah, ah,' he drawled, not attempting to conceal his pleasure, 'so the Ghost Division is in trouble again, what?'

'Sir!' the two officers agreed as one.

'Do you hear that, gentlemen,' the 5th Panzer Division Commander raised his voice so that his amused staff could hear. 'Our Swift Swabian has obviously overreached himself once more.'

There was a titter of laughter from the elegant staff officers. Major Kranz flushed angrily. 'Sir, with all due respect, the 7th Panzer Division is bleeding to death up there near Arras. Something has to be done.'

The General looked at Kranz, as if he had just crawled up out of the muddy ground all around. 'Something will be done, Major,' he said severely. 'In the 5th Panzer we never wet our knickers — unlike some commanders I might mention.' He swung round, businesslike now. 'Geil,' he rapped to the nearest staff officer, 'get on to the 15th Panzer Regiment.'

'Sir.' The staff officer poised his pencil over his pad, ready to take down the General's instructions.

'Order it to break off the action at Cambrai and launch an immediate flank attack on the Tommies. That will draw off their armour.'

'Sir.'

'Further, I want all available anti-tank batteries, which are motorized, to be sent to the aid of the 7th Panzer. Clear?'

'Clear, sir.' The officer finished scribbling down the order. Obviously in the 5th Panzer, oral orders were always recorded on paper first before being transmitted by radio, Kranz thought; unlike the Ghost Division where everything seemed to be done off the cuff. Immediately he had finished, the officer turned to the radio operator, crouched ready over his apparatus. 'Send this message,' he began, while the General turned to another aide. 'And this, immediate, to be sent via Corps HQ to the *Führer*: "7th Panzer Division cut off, 5th Panzer Division going to its assistance." ' He smiled pleasurably at his aide. 'We'll see what the Führer will think of his Swift Swabian now, what?'

At Kranz's side, von Fromm whispered, *'Ouch. Now the shit will really hit the fan!'*

Below, in the courtyard of Field Marshall von Rundstedt's Army HQ at Charleville, the watching aides could already see the *Führer*'s black Mercedes drawing up, the Leader clearly identifiable in his snuff-coloured jacket with its lone Iron Cross, sitting next to his pale-faced Chief-of-Operations General — Major Jodl. Inside the HQ, staff officers ran back and forth opening the windows to rid the place of its stink of cigars and cigarettes, while General von Sodenster, Rundstedt's Chief-of-Staff, hurriedly deposited his daily ration of schnaps bottles in his filing cabinet. They all knew Hitler's prejudices against drink and tobacco, and this surprise visit had caught them completely off guard.

Only von Rundstedt remained calm. Like a wizened old idol,

he stood by the large situation map, chain-smoking as always, waiting to receive the 'Greatest Captain of All Times' (as the National Socialist Press lauded Hitler). But then he knew the 'Bohemian Corporal', as *he* called Hitler, needed him and his strategic talent.

Hitler exchanged his usual greetings and then, putting on his steel-rimmed glasses, in which no one was ever allowed to photograph him, he followed Rundstedt to the map. Docilely he listened while the 70-year-old explained the situation in France, nodding his approval at intervals until Rundstedt came to the position of his three armoured corps in Flanders, especially that of Hoth's 15th Panzer Corps.

'Do you mean to say, Field Marshal,' he said in his hoarse Austrian voice, the note of alarm clearly detectable, 'that Rommel is cut off, and that the 5th has had to break off its action to go to his aid?'

'That is the gist of the signal I received from the 5th only thirty minutes ago, *mein Führer*,' the wizened old commander replied easily, his faded eyes revealing nothing, save perhaps mild amusement.

'But what are tanks doing in the mud of Flanders in the first place?' Hitler demanded, immediately going over to the attack, as he always did when rattled. 'I remember in the old war when I was an infantryman . . .'

Von Rundstedt closed his ears to the usual monologue. How often was he going to be plagued by the wartime experience of Lance-Corporal Hitler, he wondered?

Finally the *Führer* was finished and von Runstedt spoke coldly, ignoring completely Hitler's comments about the marshiness of the Flemish terrain. 'Speed is of the essence, if we are to trap the British before they can reach the sea, *mein Führer*.'

'But can we risk three Panzer corps — the cream of the *Wehrmacht* — to that end, Field Marshal?' Hitler protested. 'You see what has happened to Rommel. No, no, I must order the tanks stopped! Besides, there is Plan Red to be considered, the armoured thrust across the Somme into the heart of France. That is more important than the British business.' His voice rose and he swept the room full of elegant staff officers, all with the red stripe of the general staff down the side of their immaculate breeches, commandingly. 'In the end I hope and believe we will come to an agreement with Great Britain . . . *she* can rule the globe and the seas. *I* will rule Europe. Once we have made peace.'

'First we must make it, *mein Führer*. There is still the battle to be considered,' von Rundstedt reminded him softly.

'I know, I know,' Hitler snapped impatiently. 'But I am not going to risk my armour.'

'And what do you suggest, *mein Führer*?'

'The *Luftwaffe*,' Hitler answered his Commander-in-Chief promptly. 'Reichsmarschal Goering's Stukas can ensure that the British Army won't leave the continent.'

There was a murmur of protest from the assembled staff officers, which could not be quelled by Jodl's angry look.

General von Bock snapped angrily: 'It is essential that we take Dunkirk with our armour at once. If Dunkirk isn't taken, the British can transport their army anywhere – Canada, for all I know. They'll live to fight another day.'

'Yes,' another officer said hotly. 'It will be offering the Tommies a golden bridge back home.'

'Gentlemen, gentlemen,' Hitler said with unusual patience. 'The war in the West is already won. Why waste tanks doing what the *Luftwaffe* can do more economically? Don't worry, Herman Goering will finish the job.'

'It won't work, I tell you, it won't, *mein Führer*,' von Bock said angrily.

Von Rundstedt raised his frail hand with its painted, manicured nails. 'Gentlemen, you have heard what the *Führer* has just said. The *Luftwaffe* will deal with Dunkirk. We must occupy ourselves now with finally defeating the French on the other side of the Somme.' He turned to an aide, a look of absolute cynicism in his old eyes. 'Order Rommel to stop,' he commanded. 'Tell him the *Führer* thinks the war is won . . .'

*

104

'*What!*' A weary, dirty Rommel, bleeding at the temple from a shell splinter, exploded. 'What did you say?'

The radio operator swallowed hard. 'HQ says, sir, that we must halt here and re-group. We are not to press on to the coast.'

'Heaven, arse and twine!' Rommel exploded. 'When my panzers start on a journey, they have a ticket to the terminus. They don't stop half way. Ask for a confirmation of the message.'

'Sir,' the radio operator said promptly and turned back to his radio, while Rommel stared at the devastated landscape of Flanders, where in the old war, the Imperial German Army had fought for four years to make gains numbered in hundreds of metres, while now the whole French coast was open to him for the taking.

'Sir.'

He turned. It was the radio operator again. 'Yes, what does General Hoth's HQ say?' he demanded urgently.

'The same, sir. You are to halt the Division, re-group and wait for further orders.'

'Damn, damn, damn!' Rommel smashed his fist against the tank's steel side with frustrated rage, the glory on the field of battle which he had always sought vanishing before his very eyes. '*Damn!*'

'They're moving back,' the bleeding gun-layer of the sole surviving 88mm said, his voice full of awe, as if he had just seen a vision. 'The Tommies are moving back, Captain.'

Gehendges dropped the heavy shell he had been lugging from the small pile of ammunition that was all that was left. It clanged down among the glittering empty shell cases lying all around. 'What?' he croaked.

'They're buggering off.'

Gehendges slumped down suddenly, tears of relief springing up behind the pince-nez. He was safe. He had survived. He was not going to die, after all. 'I'm safe,' he cried to the dead gunners lying all about him on the shell-pitted height. 'I'm safe!'

Sergeant-Major Schott, the one survivor of the six snipers,

slogging back up the height with infinite slowness, dragging his empty rifle behind him, caught that heart-felt exclamation of relief. 'Safe,' he sneered, a whole life-time of contempt in that one word. 'Nobody's safe.'

BOOK THREE: THE LADIES FROM HELL

ONE: FÉCAMP, 10th JUNE, 1940

ONE

'A Company, East Yorks . . . HQ Yorks and Lancs . . . King's Own Scottish Borders . . . 2nd Battalion Grenadier Guards . . . Green Howards . . .'

The names of regiments and battalions that had fought the King's enemies all over the world for the last hundred years or more rang out everywhere in the darkness, as another fleet of small boats began to draw into the burning harbour.

Hurriedly, what was left of the British Expeditionary Force to France formed up under their officers and guides. Now the ack-ack was silent, for the German dive-bombers had gone for the day, and the only sound was the crunch of broken glass under the heavy, nailed boots, as if the escapees were marching over icy gravel. Occasionally the marching men caught a glimpse of some mysterious shadow flitting from doorway to doorway in the sudden flash of a German gun far off to the rear. They were the civilians who had stayed behind in Dunkirk, or the looters, who were everywhere in the bomb-proof cellars. But that was all. Now at the start of the night's embarkation schedule it seemed that the Channel port was deserted.

But that soon changed as they reached the dunes, dotted with abandoned trucks, half buried in the sand, or twisted into grotesque shapes by the previous day's shelling and bombing. Now by the light of the flames of the promenade, they could see that there were soldiers like themselves everywhere, waiting for the ships which lay somewhere at sea in the darkness that was as smooth and thick as velvet.

They started to file along the mole against the horrifying background of giant, oil-tinged scarlet flames leaping high into the air from the burning petrol refinery close by. In parties of fifty, they trudged along, tired, hungry and afraid. There was no singing now, and very little talk. Every few moments they were challenged by parties of armed, grim-faced redcaps on the look-out for individual soldiers attempting to jump the queue.

They reached the sea. At fairly wide intervals, three long thin lines of black figures stretched out into the darkness, waiting for the little boats to pick them up. There was no bunching, no pushing and no panic, even when the odd German shell plunged down among them, adding more bodies to the many nudging back and forth at the water's edge.

General Alexander, the most senior British officer in France now, sensed once again the deadly evil atmosphere of the beach as he wandered among the soldiers, munching an apple, wishing them good luck, as elegant and as casual as ever. The horrible stench of blood and mutilated flesh pervaded the whole place. It smelled to him at that moment like a slaughter-house, where the cream of British manhood was being done to death.

He stopped by a wounded man, groaning for water, and, undoing his water bottle, gently tilted up his head and gave him some.

'Thanks, mate,' the wounded soldier whispered weakly.

'That's all right, son,' the elegant Guards officer said, and lowered his head back to the wet sand. He was one, Alexander thought, who would not be going home.

Alexander had seen enough. Thrusting his way through the silent, anxious lines, he walked back to the mole, where a shed, in which an old tattered deck-chair held pride of place, served as his primitive HQ.

'What news?' he asked his aide, opening a bottle of whisky and taking a stiff drink straight from it.

'The outer perimeter line is still holding, sir,' the weary young staff officer said. 'The East Lancs, the Lincolns, the Royal West Kents — they all report they are still in a position to hold out.'

'Good.' Alexander pushed back his peaked cap. 'And casualties?'

'Terrible, sir. All battalions report their effectives down by fifty per cent.'

Alexander said nothing. He was a sensitive man, but he had

seen enough action in his time to know that a commander must just not let himself be affected by heavy casualties. 'What else?'

'The usual morning barrage is expected at six. We can also expect another dive-bombing attack at the same time. That's what air intelligence reports, anyway.'

'They're probably right. Dunkirk is wide open. I doubt we'll have enough ack-ack ammunition to last the day out.' He took another drink of the whisky bottle and yawned luxuriously. 'And what of their tanks, that damned 7th Panzer Division of theirs?'

The young aide looked at his situation map, narrowing his eyes in the white glare of the carbide lamp. 'Nothing, sir, as far as I can make out. They haven't moved for nearly four days now.'

'Thank God for that. You can thank your heathen gods, my boy!' Alexander slumped down in the battered deck-chair with its fading legend, *Plage de Dunkerque*, gratefully. 'Give me thirty-six hours more without that damned 7th Panzer attacking and they can throw in everything, including the kitchen sink. For what good it will be in the future, we will be gone.' His head dropped to one side and he was fast asleep.

Gently the aide arose and draped the one blanket they shared over him. Outside the great evacuation continued . . .

The weather was hot and still, the sky a glorious blue, with here and there a few fleeting white clouds high up. Major Kranz, lying on the turf under the tree yawned pleasurably, not even hearing the faint, ever-present rumble of the guns, staring happily at the pastoral scene. It was good to be alive, he told himself. 'Gorgeous, isn't it,' he breathed to von Fromm lying next to him.

'Probably, if you're a civilian,' his neighbour said a little grumpily, and peered through his new monocle at the fleeting clouds. 'But one doesn't get medals and promotions lying on one's arse, you know, Major.'

'I can do without them,' Kranz said easily.

'That's what war is about, you know.'

'The war's over. The *Voelkischer Beobachter*[1] says so. The Tommies are going home to play their cricket and drink tea — and the Frogs are about on their last legs.'

Von Fromm made an obscene grunt.

Kranz grinned lazily. 'You don't like it one bit that the campaign's about finished, do you, Fromm?'

'Why should I? Papa was a general, Grandpapa too. I thought I'd least make major out of this campaign and perhaps the Iron Cross First Class. I mean you civvies don't know just how hard it is to make promotion in peacetime. For example, in 1938—'

He stopped short. There was the sound of heavy trucks labouring their way in low gear up the steep lane which led to the 404th's camp. Von Fromm sat up. A long line of vehicles, towing sparklingly new 88mm flak cannon, was drawing into the laager, and in the front truck, resplendent in an immaculate new uniform was a familiar portly figure. 'Captain Gehendges and his merry men,' he announced.

Kranz sat up, too, and stared at the newcomers. 'And do you see what he's got hanging round his neck, von Fromm,' he asked a little maliciously.

'Great God and all his triangles!' von Fromm cursed, his affected drawl vanished for a moment, his eyes full of envy. 'He's got *the* piece of tin!'

'Right in one. They've given him the Knight's Cross of the Iron Cross!'

'That asparagus Tarzan — with the Knight's Cross!' von Fromm clapped his hand to his forehead in mock agony. 'Is there no justice in this world!'

Kranz grinned and sprang to his feet. 'Come on, let's see what the good Captain is doing, disturbing our little pastoral idyll, von Fromm.'

Captain Gehendges, obviously highly pleased with himself, saluted with a newly acquired casualness, and said, '6th Flak Battery reporting for attachment, sir.'

[1] Hitler's own newspaper.

Kranz returned the salute and said, 'First, my congratulations, Gehendges — on your decoration. Good work!'

Gehendges fingered the decoration, as if to reassure himself that it was still there. 'Thank you, Major. It was nothing really, but the General thought my defence of Height 222 was something of a small-action classic — or so he said, though I only did my duty,' he added modestly.

Behind Gehendges's back, the massive figure of Sergeant-Major Schott, his broad chest sporting nothing more than the black wound medal and the modest black-and-red ribbon of the Iron Cross, Third Class, seemed about to fall upon the pudgy Captain at any moment. He winked at Kranz conspiratorially and the Major smiled.

'But we got the Division out of the shit,' von Fromm complained, 'and all *we* got was an oral reproach from the General for going over his head and not going through correct channels.'

'Oh, shut up, von Fromm,' Kranz said good-humouredly. 'Everybody in the Division knows that we are on the General's personal shit-list for ever and a day. Now, Gehendges, what is this about an attachment?'

Gehendges pulled his orders out of his cuff. 'It's all in there, Major,' he said. 'But in essence, the 404th and my own battery are to form a special task for the next operation.' Kranz caught his breath. 'What operation?' he asked, puzzled. Gehendges looked at him happily. 'The attack on Fécamp.'

'*Fécamp?*'

'Yes, the village blocks the road to St Valery, the Division's major objective.' He laughed and said with his newly acquired military coarseness, 'It's our task to put the wind up the skirts of those ladies from hell.'

'*The what?*' Von Fromm and Kranz asked in unison.

'Well, that's what the General calls them. He told me the name personally.'

'But what are they?' Kranz persisted.

'The Scots — the Scottish 51st Highland Division, which holds the St Valery area. They are the ladies from hell . . .' He

115

took off his pince-nez and rubbed them clean with great deliberation. 'The Tommies managed to sneak away at Dunkirk, but the General's not going to tolerate that at St Valery. He wants the whole division — dead or alive. It's a matter of prestige with him after that nasty business at Arras. He told me personally.'

Major Kranz stared a little helplessly at the keen young faces of the reinforcements to his and Gehendges's unit. So that was what war was about. The fresh batch of cannonfodder was to be thrown into the bloody jaws of the war monster in order that the General could erase the stigma of his mistake from his personal record. It was all a matter of the General's promotion!

TWO

An ominous silence prevailed, broken only by the crash of the breakers at the bottom of the white cliffs far below, and a long, long way off, the faint rumble of many vehicles, which the waiting Scots knew belonged to the Germans.

The 4th Black Watch were ready. The coastal road was barricaded with a mess of farm carts and barrels of concrete, with barbed wire stretching to the cliff edge on one side and deep into the fields on the other side. Behind, in the pre-war boarding houses, the Jocks had dug in the cellars and further on had established machine-gun posts along the sea wall. And out to sea, glittering blindingly in the hot sun, there lay the slim shape of a British destroyer, its six 4·5-inch guns already trained on the coastal road.

Major Rory Campbell, wearing brilliant tartan trews, his copper-red hair sticking out at the side of his tam-o'shanter, was pleased. Swinging his swagger cane, he marched smartly down the cobbled street, nodding his approval, giving a word of encouragement to his Jocks, suggesting an alternative position. The Black Watch would give the Jerries a bloody nose this morning, he promised himself, or his name was nae Rory Campbell.

Then abruptly, as if some gigantic hand had thrown an invisible switch, a great flash of violent scarlet light split the bright blue of the morning sky, and shells began to descend upon the Black Watch's position.

'Hold fast, my braw laddies!' Rory Campbell yelled above the racket and dived into the nearest slit-trench. 'And save your fire till you see the whites of their eyes!' He cowered at the bottom of the pit and felt the earth shake beneath him, as if in the grip of some enormous earthquake. The Germans were coming.

The Mark IVs rumbled down the coastal road, each spread out

at the regulation distance of fifty metres, their guns swinging back and forth across their front like the snouts of predatory monsters, seeking out their prey. Their radios chattering back and forth, signalling this hedge was clear of the enemy, that ridge was unoccupied, while the new recruits' tension mounted by the moment. In the lead towing vehicle of the 88s, which had been jammed into the middle of the column to go into action as soon as any enemy tanks made their appearance (after Arras, General Rommel was being doubly careful), Schott studied the way again – and Gehendges, sitting next to him in the cab. The pudgy ex-insurance man was obviously very pleased with himself. He was playing with his Knight's Cross as if he were having a little bit of five against one, Schott couldn't help thinking. The fat Captain did not know what he was getting into, he decided.

'What do you think, sir?' he asked, as the first houses of Fécamp started to loom up out of the haze of the bombardment.

'Think?' Gehendges asked happily.

'About our attack, sir?'

'Oh, that,' Gehendges dismissed it with a wave of his pudgy hand, full of his new-found confidence. 'The General personally assured me it would be a walk-over. The heart has gone out of the Tommies. I don't doubt that they're getting ready to do a bunk just like their pals at Dunkirk. But our Stukas will see that they don't get any ships this time in which to escape. Into the bag for the 51st Scottish Division – that's the General's aim.' He beamed at Schott, 'Don't—'

He stopped short. There was a strange look on the big NCO's red, honest face. 'What is it?' he asked in sudden alarm, the smile gone abruptly.

Schott did not answer. He was staring at the dark figure which had suddenly risen from a ditch about two hundred metres away, a long object which could have been a farmer's pole on his shoulder but which he knew instinctively wasn't.

In the same instant that the dark figure flung himself and the anti-tank rifle down, Schott grabbed the wheel from the startled driver and wrenched it to the right. Just in time. As the big towing vehicle smashed into one of the poplars which lined the sun-drenched road, its gun jack-knifing behind it, the solid 55mm anti-tank bullet hissed by them in a white blur and smacked into the windscreen of the vehicle behind, taking the driver's head with it. Completely out of control, the towing vehicle shot off the road and overturned on the steep embankment, wrapping itself and the big gun in a confused mess of wrecked metal and groaning, screaming soldiers.

That lone shot seemed to act as a signal. With a great whoosh, the six naval guns of the destroyer opened up and missed the road by metres, showering the tanks and trucks with a great rain of mud and gravel, shaking them violently so that it seemed for a moment as if they would be blown off the elevated road.

Kranz caught his breath. He gripped the side of the turret wildly, catching himself from falling just in time.

'Sir, watch your arse — *sir!*' von Fromm's voice screamed a frantic warning.

He spun round, head still ringing with the effect of that first tremendous blast. A khaki-clad figure had risen from the ditch towards his rear and was doubling madly towards his tank, a small, bell-shaped object held in his hands.

'Sticky grenade!' von Fromm enlightened him. 'He's got a sticky grenade!'

Kranz swung the turret m.g. round and fired in the same instant. The Tommy went down, his spine arched, the object falling as his hands were suddenly flung towards the burning heavens, as if pleading for mercy.

'Whew,' his driver breathed. 'Look at that!'

Kranz forgot the bomber. He turned to his front. Ahead, the whole village of Fécamp had erupted in violent fire. Tracer zig-zagged through the air. Instinctively he ducked as the first slugs whined off the turret, howling off into the distance. As the next salvo from the destroyer howled down, burrowing up huge bursts of earth in front of the advancing column, Kranz knew with a sinking heart that they were in for a fight, a bloody, awful fight.

*

Kranz crouched next to Gehendges in the ditch. Now the new-won bravado was gone. The trembling, ashen-faced man next to him was the old Gehendges, a frightened, middle-aged civilian who would have given the world at this moment to be able to return to Cologne and his *petite-bourgeois* existence.

'Listen,' he lectured the other man, as if he were a small and stupid child. 'That damn Tommy destroyer out there is going to stop every attack we can raise, and we've no infantry to try it another way. So, we've got to knock out that destroyer.'

He waited for some reaction from Gehendges, but he waited in vain. The Captain was too preoccupied with his fear. In the end, Sergeant-Major Schott spoke for him. 'You mean, sir,' he prompted, 'you want Captain Gehendges's battery to tackle the boat?'

'Exactly.'

'It's going to be tough, sir,' Schott said thoughtfully. 'The Tommies have got snipers out there everywhere and our towing vehicles, as you know, are not armoured.'

'It's a chance you have got to take, at least until you find a site to set up your guns. I'll give you a couple of my crews to act as covering infantry. Von Fromm, you pick a half-dozen men and lead them yourself.'

'You mean act as a common stubble-hopper?' von Fromm reacted with mock horror. 'You know, sir, I haven't marched since my training days. I doubt if my delicate feet will know what to do!'

'Well, now's the time to find out,' Kranz grinned. Then his grin vanished as he realized once again the seriousness of their situation. 'All right, get on with it. Gehendges and you, von Fromm, will move out in ten minutes. I'll plaster the village with 75mm fire. Off with you now.'

'Nothing must stop the Guard!' von Fromm cried cheerfully. 'And remember, sir, keep your eye on me. If you see me doing anything heroic, get it down on paper. I need *that* tin.'

'*Suicide squad!*' von Fromm commanded, instantly recognizing the little group of khaki-clad men who had sprung up from the ditch to his front and were racing after the leading vehicle, for what they were.

Next to him, the man carrying the spandau machine gun raised it. Without any command, his number two bent and accepted the heavy barrel on his right shoulder. The gunner pressed the trigger. It burst into hysterical, high-pitched life.

The leading Tommy skidded to a stop and slapped down on the cobbles, his back ripped open. Another followed him, blood-red holes stitched the length of his shoulders like the work of some sadistic tailor. But the third man managed to avoid the burst. Next moment, von Fromm could hear the hollow clang of the sticky grenade being attached to the side of the towing vehicle. He cupped his hands around his mouth and yelled, 'Stop . . . stop!' In vain. The towing vehicle rolled forward, von Fromm's cries drowned by the roar of the motor in low gear.

Schott saw the danger too. He hit the horn of his truck. 'Wake up, you stupid barn-shitters!' he bellowed, his face crimson, while Gehendges cowered next to him, 'you've got a cuckoo's egg up your arse! Wa—'

There was a thick asthmatic cough. The truck reared up in the air, flinging bodies to both sides like sacks of cement. The axle burst, spraying hot oil everywhere, while the gun zig-zagged to left and right, breaking the towing hook and smashing into the ditch, its barrel burying deep into the earth. Gun number one was out of action.

Schott sprang out of the truck, machine pistol in his big hands. Another Tommy suicide squad was running towards the gunners, frantically attempting to uncouple the 88mm. Standing like a cowboy in a pre-war Western, legs spread apart, he swept the m.p. from side to side, hosing the running men with slugs. They were swept aside, as if they had never even existed. A bullet smacked into the side of the cab, millimetres away from his head.

'Sniper!' somebody sang out.

'Sniper!' Gehendges quavered and sank to his knees.

Schott grabbed him roughly by the neck. 'Get your yellow

121

arse up!' he bellowed. 'Cover me—' his words were drowned by the scream of one of the gunners, as the sniper's slug smashed the base of his skull. 'Cover me, I'm going to get that sneaky Tommy bastard!'

With fingers that trembled like leaves in a strong wind, Gehendges pulled out his pistol and attempted to point it, while Schott dived into the underground that lined the cliff's edge and started to crawl in the direction of the last shot.

Major Rory Campbell saw the danger immediately. Lowering his binoculars from the German trucks and their cannon, he bit his bottom lip, trying to out-think the Jerries. Obviously they were going to use the long-barrelled, heavy cannon of a type he had never seen before, to knock out the destroyer or at least to force it to withdraw further out. Once the 4th Black Watch had lost the protection of the ship's guns, the Jerries would attack with their tanks, and the Boyes Rifle[1] was about as useful as a pea-shooter against the Jerry armour. They would be easy meat for the enemy.

'Sandy,' he snapped at the craggy-faced, ancient corporal standing next to him, his right arm covered almost to the elbow with long-service stripes.

'Ay,' Corporal Sandy Sanders growled with a voice oiled by years of cheap whisky. 'Ye want me to keep yon Huns occupied, I fancy?'

'Exactly.'

'What's in it fer me?' the veteran of World War One, the North-West Frontier, and a half a hundred other campaigns, grunted. 'Ye know, the Sanders dinna do a thing fer nothin'.'

'A forty-eight to Edinburgh when we get back over there and as much whisky as you can sup, Sandy.'

'That sounds no bad, but I could do with a wee dram before I go, ye ken, Major.'

'*Major!*' Rory Campbell said in mock amazement, 'You even deign to address your commanding officer by his rank. Things

[1] Anti-tank rifle, firing an armour-piercing bullet.

must be bad.' He pulled the silver flask out of his hip pocket, unscrewed it, and handed it to the expectant Corporal.

Sandy took it into his big gnarled hands, as if he were handling the Holy Grail itself. 'Ye know it's only for medicinal purposes, Major,' he said, throat thick with greed, and raised it to his parched old lips.

'Ay, pull the other one, Sandy, its got bells on it!'

The ancient Corporal, who was the Division's best shot, was no longer listening. His whole attention was concentrated on the contents of the flask. Raising it to its fullest extent, he poured the last drops of the fiery fluid down his throat.

'My God,' Major Campbell breathed in awe, 'that's a whole gill which you've put into your raddled old guts! Good grief, man, I wouldn't even be able to see the target with that load aboard.'

Sandy wiped his mouth carefully. 'Ay, but youse you, and I'm me.' He slung his Lee Enfield with its telescopic sight. 'I'll be on my way then. A good day to ye, Major.'

And with that Sandy Sanders disappeared into the undergrowth, his little red eyes burning with all-consuming rage.

Schott saw the sniper in the same instant that the sniper, his face, streaked a crazy mixture of black and brown paint, spotted him. The Lee Enfield cracked. A bullet cut through the grass to his side. Schott sprang to his feet. He knew this was his only chance. Crazily the sniper worked his bolt, ejected the cartridge case, and slammed home another slug. But Schott was quicker. His machine pistol scythed the trees with bullets. The sniper screamed, his guts suddenly ripped open, and smashed to the ground fifteen metres below, his body bouncing up with the impact and then slamming down one more time to lie completely still.

Schott breathed out hard. That had been a close one. He had almost walked right into the sniper's trap. Only the fact that the crows, which had risen and then wanted to settle again after the last salvo of naval fire had not attempted to land on that particular tree, had alerted him to the presence of a human being hidden there. For a minute he just stood there, controlling his nerves, before telling himself he would scout around a little more. There might be other snipers about and he did not want to lose any more of his young gunners to a sudden slug in the back. Slipping another magazine into his Schmeisser, he skirted the sniper's crumpled body, completely unaware of the old, hard-faced Corporal lying only five metres away, intent on a better target than the lone German.

'*Fire!*'' Gehendges roared.

The gun-layer pulled the firing bar. The 88mm cracked into life. Its shell tore the air apart. One thousand metres away, there was an abrupt burst of wild, boiling-white water just to the destroyer's sharp bow.

'*Up fifty!*' Gehendges corrected automatically.

'*Up fifty,*' the gun commander echoed, as the layer whirled his wheels and made his adjustments.

'*In!*' the loader snapped, thrusting home the big, gleaming shell.

'*On,*' the gun-layer barked and waited.

'*Fire!*'

Again the big gun thundered. Churning seawater, white and green, drenched the destroyer's foredeck, sending her reeling back and forth like a toy boat in a bath.

'Excellent . . . *excellent!*' Gehendges cried, already visualizing being presented with his next decoration by the *Führer* himself. There'd be a parade in Berlin in his honour and then the girls in their sheer black silk stockings . . . He forced himself to concentrate on the task in hand. '*Same range!*' he bellowed as the destroyer began its counter-fire. 'Hurry it up now. It isn't every day that a flak gun shoots down a destroyer, is it?'

He smiled at his own humour.

Sandy Sanders wormed his way through the scrub, sniper's rifle lying across his arms, moving easily and soundlessly towards the unsuspecting Germans, that old, old rage burning within him. All his life, ever since his days as a ragged-arsed kid in the

Gorbals, he had been angry at something or somebody – the dominie at school, the parish priest, the drill sergeant, the wogs, his 'old lady' – and the only way he had ever found to overcome his anger had been to strike out.

His temper had taken him from the reformatory into the Army and there into cells and glasshouses over half the world. He had become what old sweats liked to call 'a hard case'. In peacetime, his temper had been confined to 'getting the boot in' in the wet canteen on paynight when he'd spent his pay on drink. But in wartime, it made of him a killer. Now Sandy Sanders, the oldest soldier in the 4th Black Watch, was out to kill.

From his hiding place he watched the sweating Jerry gun crew objectively, assessing the possibilities like some grand English 'sport' out for the shooting in the glens. The officer, he decided. He must go. He was an obvious choice. Who next? He reasoned that he'd get in at least two shots before they began to react. In the end, he concluded the loader was the next one. The officer and the loader – they'd be the two. Carefully he began to sight his rifle until the officer's sweating pudgy face slid into the bright gleam circle of calibrated glass.

'Fire, men!' Gehendges yelled joyfully. 'We've got the Tommy bastards on the run!' He raised his voice even higher. 'They're going. Let's get them!'

The destroyer, its side gouged a shining metallic grey where the 88's shells had struck it, its radio mast hanging down drunkenly, severed by a lucky shot, was making steam. Already the white water was beginning to curl at its bow. Obviously the 88s were proving too much for it.

Now Gehendges's courage was returning. What headlines the event would make back in the Reich! *Artillery Captain drives off enemy destroyer*. It would be the making of him. It would make his fortune.

'Come on, you lazy pack of good-for-nothings, get to it, will you!' he commanded and rammed his boot into the skinny behind of the gun-layer. 'Move it!'

*

125

'Yon feller needs taking down a wee peg or two,' Sandy Sanders said, speaking to himself in the manner of many lonely men. 'And I think our Sandy is just the feller to do it for him.' He nestled the butt of the Lee Enfield into his shoulder tightly and took aim until the black foresight parted the fat officer's head in two, just behind the right ear. Almost lovingly he pressed the trigger. A slight jerk, a slap against his shoulder and the bullet was winging its way across the two hundred yards to put a sudden end to Captain Gerhardt Gehendges's dreams for ever.

Gehendges pitched to the ground, his eyes full of stark, uncomprehending horror that this was happening to him, fat Gerhardt of the *Colonia Insurance AG*, the man who had dreamed all his life of giggling half-naked whores in sheer black silk stockings. He hit the earth and was dead in the same instant that the destroyer finally took the bone between her teeth and headed for the open sea, followed by the cheers of the triumphant gun crew, which ended abruptly in cries of panic when Sandy Sanders's rifle spoke again.

Major Kranz read the cheers correctly. Gehendges had pulled it off! He had driven the destroyer away. Not waiting for von Fromm to return, he waved his hand above his head at the waiting tank crews. They knew immediately what he meant. Start up.
    Everywhere the drivers hit the starter buttons. The air was flooded with blue smoke. The noise shattered the silence of the hollow behind the road in which they were hidden. Kranz pressed his throat mike and uttered one word, '*Attack!*'

THREE

Major Campbell looked around at his men as the enemy 75mms crashed down in yet another volley. Some were wild-eyed and quivering under the strain. Near the buckled crane, which dripped molten metal to the quay, a young private sobbed broken-heartedly, while next to him a sergeant, his guts ripped open so that his intestines hung out on the ground, cried weakly, 'Come on and fight fair, you bloody Jerry bastards!'

He scuttled to a corporal who had just been hit and was writhing in the dust, a hole in his chest and his arm shattered, hanging on by a thread. The Major thrust a dirty handkerchief in the chest wound to give some sort of halt to the blood pouring from it and then, wiping his bloody hands on his tartan trews, once his pride but now virtually ripped to shreds, he pulled out his jack knife. He honed the blade swiftly on the instep of his boot, tested it for sharpness and then without any further ado, took off what was left of the arm. Improvising a tourniquet with the man's handkerchief and a pencil, he left the soldier to survive as best he could. Now he could hear the rumble of their tanks getting ever louder. Soon they would hit the first line of defence and he wanted to be there when they did. Ignoring the shrapnel flying everywhere, hissing through the air in frightening red-hot shards, he ran towards the first barricade. 'All right, laddies, stand fast — here they come!' he cried.

Sandy Sanders lay out in no-man's land completely relaxed. Concealed in a clump of thick coastal shrub, he watched the German tanks rumble forward with professional detachment. Indeed at that particular moment, his mind was really concentrated on the whisky the Major had promised him. He licked his cracked lips in pleasurable anticipation and then, as the first tank drew closer and closer, he started to make his decision how to tackle it.

He could see that it was buttoned down. The commander was being careful. He was watching his front through the periscope, safe behind the thick armour. Sandy grinned, though there was nothing nice about that grin. His little red eyes remained as angry as ever. He studied the movement of the periscope in the turret and raised his rifle. Through the telescopic lens, he could make it out quite clearly. He lowered the rifle. The driving compartment slid into view. He could make out the white blur of the driver's face easily. 'Ay, ma wee laddie,' he said to himself, 'ye think yer safe behind yon bit of tin. But ye no ken Sandy Sanders, I ween.'

The ancient, leather-faced Corporal made his decision. He took careful aim and squeezed the trigger. The first bullet smashed right into the periscope; the second hissed through the driver's slit and drilled him neatly through the forehead. The Mark IV went out of control immediately. Shorn of vision and driverless, it shot off the road, screeching and lurching down the steep embankment to crash on its back below like some obscene great metallic beetle.

Sandy Sanders smiled bleakly to himself. 'No bad,' he muttered to himself and slipped another magazine into his Lee Enfield. 'No bad at all.'

'Off the road, off the shitty road!' Kranz bellowed, as he saw the wrecked tank through a break in the thick brown smoke which billowed across the battlefield.

'But sir!' the driver protested.

'No buts,' Kranz cried, 'move it!' He turned to the gunner. 'Spray the whole shitty front with m.g. fire. There's a sniper out there somewhere!'

The young soldier needed no urging. He knew from the tales of the old soldiers what could happen if a sniper's bullet penetrated the turret and began hissing back and forth on the armoured walls like a crazy hornet. His machine gun chattered at once, filling the cupola with acrid smoke, as the driver selected the spot where he would leave the high, elevated coastal road.

He saw it and raced through the Mark IV's twenty-odd gears, bringing the engine down to almost stalling speed. 'Hold tight!' he cried over the intercom and tilted the nose over the side of the road. In that same instant, Sandy Sanders's slug slammed into the glacis plate, only millimetres away from his face. Instinctly the frightened, tousled-haired driver closed his eyes. With a frightening lurch, the Mark IV went over the side. He hit the brakes. Gravel and mud showered up on both sides like the wake of a speeding ship.

'Hold it, for God's sake!' Kranz yelled in alarm.

'Trying to, sir!' the driver screamed back, fighting the controls, his body breaking out in a hot sweat. A thrill of fear shot through him. The 20-ton monster was beginning to rock alarmingly, as it slithered down the steep slope. With all his strength, the driver threw the clutch across the bar, hoping desperately it would engage. It did. The furious roar of the overworked engine quietened a little. But the tank was still sliding.

'Ease on the brakes!' Kranz ordered.

The confused driver applied the brakes to both tracks. The tank's furious progress continued. In an instant, it would overturn.

'The left track, you shitty-assed idiot!' Kranz screamed. *'The left track!'*

The driver jammed down the brake which stopped the left track. The Mark IV swung violently round. For one awful moment, Kranz thought they would overturn. The tank shuddered in every rivet, as if it were falling apart, and then the tracks gripped. One second later, with every man in the crew soaked in sweat and trembling all over, it bumped safely to the bottom of the steep incline, leaving the rest of the column, stalled and undecided, on the road above them.

'Ah, lovely grub!' Sanders breathed, as tank after tank came to a halt at the stop where the second Mark IV had disappeared over the side of the road. 'Now, ma wee German laddies, Sandy

129

Sanders is going to put a few lead bees up yer kilts fer ye.' He raised his rifle in pleasurable anticipation.

A burst of machine pistol fire sprayed the bushes all around him with the sound of heavy tropical rain drumming down on a tin roof. Sandy reacted immediately. Rolling on his back, he flung himself a metre away from where he had just been, pumped off three unaimed shots, and dived to his right into another bush.

Von Fromm cursed and ducked as the slugs hissed over his head. He had thought he had the Tommy sniper with his knickers down, but the ancient bastard had proved wilier and quicker than he had anticipated. For a moment he hesitated. The side of the road was covered in a thick scrub as far as the eye could see. The sniper, obviously a highly trained one at that, could be anywhere. He could not afford to risk his men's lives, trying to beat him out. But he knew, too, that if the Tommy was not knocked out, he'd drill a hole in every driver's head in the stalled tanks above. It was an agonizing decision to make, but he made it as the von Fromms had always made such decisions on the battlefield. 'All right, you lot, stay here. Anything moves in khaki — blast a big hole in it. It won't be me.' He took a deep breath. 'Nothing must stop the Guard!' he yelled, and dived into the shrubs. Von Fromm's private war had commenced.

Kranz's driver whirled round the slit trench, round and round, tracks flailing, mud showering high in the air. The sides began to give. 'One more time,' Kranz cried.

The driver spun the tank round. Below, the pit gave way. The right track bit deep into the terrified men cowering there, churning them in an instant to bloody pulp, flooding the bottom of the trench with their steaming blood.

'Advance!' Kranz ordered and the tank shot forward, one lone arm flopping back and forth in its axle, as it headed for the next Tommy position.

Now slugs whined off the tank from all sides. A hail of fire came from the barricaded houses, as the Black Watch desperately tried to stop the monster which had appeared in their midst so alarmingly. Kranz did not seem to notice, though his young crew jumped visibly every time a fresh volley struck the tank's metal sides. His gaze was searching for the Tommy command post. Shoot that up and he'd have them on the run. Without its brain, the enemy would be powerless.

'Bomber!' the gunner screamed and fired. The stream of tracer hissed by the running man, splattering into the wall opposite. The man with the Molotov Cocktail in his upraised hand came on running.

'Hit him, for God's sake,' Kranz ordered.

'A stoppage, I've got a stoppage somewhere!' the gunner yelled back, frantically trying to unlock the jammed breech.

Now the Tommy was only a matter of metres away. He prepared to throw. Kranz could see his chest expand as he took a deep breath. The Major flung back the turret hatch. Bullets hissed through the air all around him. From both sides of the street, the Tommies in the upper windows took aim at the new target. Kranz did not notice. His eyes were fixed on the running man. As if back on some peacetime range, he took careful aim with his pistol. It barked once, twice. The running man's knees buckled beneath him. The bottle fell from his nerveless hand. Next instant it had exploded. In a flash he was wreathed in bright blue flames, screaming hideously, as he disappeared behind the burning wall, illuminating as he did the crude wooden sign to his immediate right, 'HQ, 4th B. Watch'.

'Swing right, driver,' Kranz gasped and dropped behind the cover of the turret. He had seen the enemy's command post.

The driver swung the tank round. He crunched over the burning man and rumbled into a tight side street.

Cautiously von Fromm raised his helmet on a twig held in his left hand, his right hand gripping the machine pistol, ready to fire at once.

Nothing happened. The Tommy sniper had not fallen for the old trick.

He cursed, and allowed the helmet to sink. All he had done

was to give away his own position. Hurriedly he threw himself to one side and began to crawl away from the spot where he had halted, seconds before the bullet howled into the undergrowth. He had missed death by a hair's breath.

It was now fifteen minutes since he had gone into the bushes to winkle out the sniper and on both occasions when he had been firmly convinced he had trapped the man, the Tommy had managed to escape. Or was he trying to escape? The question thrilled through his brain alarmingly. Was it possible that the Tommy was luring him deeper and deeper into the scrub, away from the rest of the men, in order to finish him off in peace?

Von Fromm paused in his crawling, his heart beating furiously with sudden alarm, realizing for the first time what a dangerous mission he had undertaken. He might have youth and strength on his side against this ancient Tommy, but the sniper had the cold-blooded cunning of the old soldier's on his. What was he to do?

Von Fromm did not have much time to consider that question. A slug howled frighteningly through the bushes and smashed right into the Schmeisser. He yelped with pain, as the machine pistol rammed into his side. The bastard had found the abandoned helmet and had trailed him towards his present hiding place. Angrily he lifted the m.p. and attempted to fire an angry burst into the undergrowth. Nothing happened! He flashed a look down at the machine pistol. The magazine holder was buckled, a gleaming, metallic hole drilled through it. Fear shot through him. The bullet had fused the bullets within the magazine into a mess of rock-hard brass and steel. The whole mechanism was jammed. With a curse he flung the m.p. into the bushes and began to crawl rapidly to his rear. He was now completely defenceless against the hidden sniper.

Sandy Sanders's craggy face creased into a leathery smile as he picked up the wrecked machine pistol. 'Weel, laddie, now that's a wee bit too bad, 'ain't it. Ye no have yer little pop-gun now.' He slipped back the bolt of his rifle to check whether the slug was still in place and then followed von Fromm's trail, the blood-lust burning in his little eyes. Sandy Sanders was going in for the kill.

Rory Campbell, hatless, his face streaked with blood, sweat and dirt, raged inwardly. Half the battalion had gone now. The massed fire of the Jerry tanks had done the trick. And now one of the bastards was loose in Fécamp, shooting up house after house unopposed.

'Sir?' It was the company runner Macintosh, a Glasgow Jew who had once been called Rosenstein.

'What is it, Rosie?' he demanded, putting his pistol back in its holster.

'They're moving back on the coastal road again. Ten Mark IVs. Our boys couldn't hold them.'

'Blast and damn!' Campbell cursed. Sandy and the rest were obviously dead.

'What are we going to do, sir?' the runner asked anxiously.

'Do you . . .?'

There was great tearing noise. A shell slammed into the side of the house. Plaster dust fell in a thick grey rain, tiles clattered to the cobbles, and someone screamed.

'Great balls of fire!' Major Campbell cried, staring through the suddenly shattered window. A German tank was only fifty yards away, the smoke curling from the end of its cannon, its crew oblivious to the bullets smacking into their armoured sides and howling off into space uselessly. And it was clear that it would soon fire again.

'Get the hell out of here,' Major Campbell ordered, 'at the double. D'yer hear, lads!'

Madly the HQ staff scrambled to the backdoor to be blown back the next instant by a tank shell exploding in the yard. Men went down screaming everywhere.

'What is it, Rosie?' Campbell cried, as the runner staggered inside again, blood streaming from a shoulder wound.

'Two of them——' the runner caught the table-edge to steady himself, '——two others have come in from the back. They've . . . they've got the whole street under control, sir.'

133

Rory Campbell, his command now disintegrating by the minute, pressed himself against the kitchen wall, as the first tank fired once more, and considered what he should do. But even before he started he knew what his decision would be. He was trapped, and probably the same thing was happening to his men, dug in their strongpoints all over the village, too. Could he let his Jocks be slaughtered to no purpose by the Jerries? He knew he could not. They had suffered enough. Then what was it going to be – surrender or withdrawal?

Withdrawal! What was left of the 4th Black Watch were going to live to fight another day. Campbell grabbed the Very pistol from its holster hanging from the shattered wall. He doubled up the stairs which shook and trembled underneath him as the tank began to shoot up the command post systematically. He emerged onto the top floor and stopped short. The whole of one wall was gone, the great brass bed which had once dominated the room half hanging out into space. Beyond the German tanks with their sinister black crosses were scuttling about everywhere like evil black beetles, spraying the house tops with machine-gun fire, stopping at regular intervals to let some particularly obstinate Jock strongpoint have a round of 75mm fire at the closest possible range.

Campbell knew the 4th Black Watch had not got much time left. They had to get out of Fécamp at once. He paused at the edge of the shattered wall and raised the signal pistol.

Kranz's gunner spotted him immediately. The red-haired officer's trousers, tattered as they were, stood out easily against the grey facade of the house. He swung the turret m.g. up in the same moment that Kranz saw the British officer poised there, Very pistol in his hand.

'Hold it, perhaps he's going to surrender—'

Too late. The gunner pressed the trigger. Tracer stitched through the smoke. The figure on the edge of the ruined wall staggered violently, his knees crumpling beneath him. For a moment he tottered there like a drunken man. The flare gun exploded in his hand, sending the red and green order to retreat hissing into the burning sky in the same instant that Major Rory Campbell plummeted to the ground.

Von Fromm wriggled cautiously through the rubble of what had obviously been a barn. Even after years of being abandoned, it still stank of animals. Above him he saw the blackened, ancient timbers, marked still by the knives of the men who had carved them. Carefully, trying to make as little noise as possible – for he guessed the sniper could not be very far behind him – he reached up, and, with a little grunt, hauled himself upwards and onto the middle beam. Lying full length there, hoping his slim body was not showing, he pulled the heavy stone out of his pocket where he had hidden it a moment before, feeling that moment like David about to tackle Goliath. A stone against a killer armed with a high-power sniper's rifle!

He caught his breath. There was a soft footfall from outside. It was the sniper. He clutched the stone more tightly. He could have one chance – and one only. '*Nothing can stop the Guard*', he whispered to himself, but there was no confidence left in his voice. This, he knew, was what the Spaniards called the 'moment of truth'.

There it was again – the soft sound of a foot being placed down with extreme care. Was it his imagination, or had he just heard the soft click of a rifle bolt being thrust home? A shadow slid across the pile of stone rubble that littered the entrance to the barn. It was the sniper all right!

Von Fromm swallowed hard. His every nerve was tensed. If he did not get in the first blow, he was finished. His hand clutching the heavy stone formed a sweat-wet claw.

'Come on, ye Hun bastard, take it!' the incredibly ancient-looking man sprang through the door, firing as he came. The slugs whined about the barn frighteningly. Almost before he knew what he had done, von Fromm flung the heavy stone. It caught the sniper's shoulder. He growled with pain and the rifle clattered to the floor. In an instant, von Fromm had dropped from the beam and was on him. The sniper went down, his little red-eyes glittering up at von Fromm in burning rage. Madly the two of them writhed and scuffled in the ancient dust. Twice the sniper tried to bring his knee up into von Fromm's groin and twice the German avoided him. Suddenly the sniper went limp in von Fromm's hands. He relaxed his guard for an instant. At once, the little man's two fingers shot up and drove deep into his nostrils. Von Fromm screamed, as the sniper curled them up with his nose and began to rip outwards. His eyes flooded with tears of absolute pain, as the blood streamed down his chin. Crazily he writhed back and forth, trying to free himself, and only succeeded in driving those terribly cruel fingers ever deeper into his nose. It felt as if it would be ripped apart at any moment. Beneath him the sniper gasped in triumph and held on with all his strength, while von Fromm's hands beat the earth in absolutely unbearable pain.

Suddenly his right hand came in contact with something cold and hard. *The stone!* The stone he had used against the man. With the last of his strength, feeling himself about to black out at any second, he smashed it against the little man's triumphant face.

Sanders screamed as his face cracked like egg-shell, his false teeth bulging out of his mouth obscenely. Still he held on. Von Fromm panicked. He must free himself. Black-red mists were threatening to overcome him. He crashed the stone into the sniper's face again. The man's nose snapped. He could hear it break. In a flash his wizened face disappeared in a spurt of bubbling crimson. Von Fromm hit him again and again. The two fingers slipped out of his nose with a wet plop.

The German did not even notice that the pain had vanished. Nor did he see that Sandy Sanders was already dead. He was overcome by a burning blood-red rage that wanted one thing only — to batter and batter the wrecked face into a red pulp. Time and time again he smashed the blood-wet stone into that dead face until it was an unrecognizable mess and all strength had fled from his limbs. Sobbing wildly, his chest heaving like that of some ancient asthmatic, he staggered to the door and leaned weakly there, seeing nothing, hearing nothing, feeling nothing, a great emptiness filling his young mind.

Then he began to stumble his way across the clifftop towards Fécamp, leaving behind the smashed body of Sandy Sanders, who had died the way he had lived — brutally and without remorse. But that ancient 'hard case' would never be forgotten by Captain von Fromm. The young aristocrat would carry the horrifying memory of that day with him to the end of his life. From now onwards the victim and murderer would be linked inseparably, like two star-crossed lovers.

Major Kranz took a deep pull of the looted bottle of cognac, feeling the fiery spirit burn and tear its way down his parched gullet and not caring, grateful for anything which would make the sight of death and destruction all around him in the captured village hazy and less immediate, dampening the bloody bruality of total war.

Sergeant-Major Schott waited dutifully. He had already drunk a half a bottle of looted spirits himself, though no one would have noticed save for the slightly wet gleam of his bright blue eyes. Finally Kranz tossed the bottle onto the still smoking cobbles where it splintered with a slight crack that made the still nervous troopers lying exhausted all around, tremble. 'Well, Sergeant-Major,' he said thickly, 'what news have you for me?'

'Captain Gehendges is dead. Ten more effectives bought. Three cannon, too.'

'I see,' Kranz said, his voice remote, his eyes elsewhere, as if he could not bear to look at what had happened in the shattered village. 'You'd better place yourself under my command for the time being.'

'Sir!' the Sergeant-Major said happily. He liked the young Major. Kranz was no glory-hunter. He felt he could work well together with him. 'And your orders, sir?'

'Orders?' Kranz echoed uncertainly, as if he were very puzzled, 'why I haven't really—'

'*Orders?*' a familiar voice cut into his deliberations, loud, clear and very definitely Swabian, as the staff car skidded to a halt.

'I'll tell you your orders, Major,' General Rommel cried, his bright eyes dancing with barely controlled excitement. 'The ladies from hell have picked up their skirts and are running for it to St Valery.' Standing upright in the car, pointing his cane like some ancient Roman emperor in his chariot, he commanded imperiously, 'On to St Valery. *The Ghost Division will drive them into the sea . . .*'

TWO: ST VALERY, 12th JUNE, 1940

ONE

Now the whole of the 51st Highland Division was falling back. The Argylls had stood their ground for as long as they could. But now the Gordons were forced to withdraw in order to avoid being outflanked. The Argylls had to follow. The 4th Black Watch was ordered to counter-attack. A squadron of French tanks was to support them. The French tanks did not appear and the counter-attack was a failure. The 4th Black Watch pulled back, too.

For a while the Scots Fusiliers held the river line, but German heavy guns covered a massive infantry attack and the Fusiliers were forced to retire. Now everywhere the survivors, some battalions down to company strength, were pulling into St Valery itself. The pride of Scotland, its Highland Division, was about to fight its last battle.

General Fortune, big, burly, moustached, his uniform looking too small for his massive frame, poked his cane at the map propped up on the blackboard of the little school which served as his divisional HQ and said: 'According to Intelligence, the Hun has seized the high ground here, to the west. That means he can bring the whole port under fire.'

The grave-faced staff officers nodded their understanding. They all knew what the announcement meant, but no one spoke.

'At present, however, the Hun is not making use of the high ground. Most of the fighting seems to be going on here at Le Tot and over here on the St Sylvain—St Valery road. Behind the port — here — we have a very strong position on the high ground.' He forced a smile. 'The fighting is in the cemetery, to be exact. Hopefully the local grave-diggers will be handy to bury a few Boche for us.'

There was a polite titter of laughter at the General's weak attempt at humour. The steady rumble of the barrage outside

141

would not let the officers forget their situation was desperate, and Scots are not given to humour in desperate situations.

Fortune frowned and continued. 'Now, it is my guess that once the Boche clears up the trouble at Le Tot, and undoubtedly that won't take long because our chaps can't do much against his tanks, he'll launch a massive attack from the heights to the west, probably under cover of a barrage. At all events, gentlemen, that is where I am going to locate the mass of the infantry. Trying to read the mind of this chap Rommel, I suspect he'll attack there and try to break through to the harbour to cut us off from the sea.' He paused and looked around his officers' grave, tired faces, knowing that he owed them an explanation. He tugged the end of his moustache, almost as if he were embarrassed, and continued. 'Now, I know what you are thinking, gentlemen. You're asking yourselves, why did we have to be landed here in the first place when the powers-that-be had already decided to evacuate the BEF at Dunkirk? What purpose were we to serve? And you are also asking yourselves, what purpose are we serving here now? Why aren't *we* being evacuated, too?' He licked his dry lips. 'Frankly, I don't know, gentlemen. Perhaps those chaps in London do. The Frocks,' he used the First World War nickname for the politicians, 'could have some scheme for us. But what it could be at this, the eleventh hour, when it is pretty obvious that the French have had it, God only knows.' His voice hardened. 'All I know, gentlemen, is this. The 51st Division will fight to the end or until London, in the fullness of time, decides we are to be evacuated. Now all depends on the Hun – and Mr Churchill. Gentlemen, good morning.'

England's new premier, Churchill, spoke slowly and carefully, hammering his words together in a vivid mosaic. He told the sallow-faced French Prime Minister Reynaud and his advisers that the two allies had to face up to the realities of the situation in this grave hour. Every effort was being made in Britain to re-equip the troops who had been evacuated at Dunkirk. At this very moment a Canadian division was landing in France and the

142

51st Division was already in action against the Germans. France must hold out until Britain could re-enter Europe again with its re-organized Army.

Reynaud shrugged his shoulders with a Gallic gesture of despair. 'Driblets, Monsieur Churchill,' he said contemptuously, facing the bluff old Englishman in the fading light of the hot June day. 'We have not a single battalion in reserve. The whole of the French Army is engaged in battle. The troops fight all day, then fall back to new positions during the night. The men have neither food nor rest. They collapse into sleep when halted and have to be shaken by their officers in the morning to open fire.' He nodded to the ancient Commander-In-Chief, Marshal Weygand, and lit a cigarette, his hand trembling. 'Tell him, Marshal,' he ordered.

Weygand turned to Churchill. 'It is a race between the exhaustion of the French and the shortness of breath of the enemy divisions,' he said. 'There is nothing to prevent the enemy reaching Paris now. We are fighting on our last line and *it* has already been breached.' His calm, expostulatory tone vanished abruptly. 'I am helpless. I can't intervene because I have no reserves. *C'est la dislocation* – the break up . . . Indeed, I wish to put on record that I consider that those responsible embarked upon this war very lightly—'

'Be quiet, Marshal!' Churchill interrupted brutally in his heavily accented French, his face flushed with anger. Turning away from Weygand, as if he never wished to see him again, he said to Reynaud, 'Give me four weeks, Prime Minister. Hold for one month, and I promise you that I will have sufficient British troops in France on the coast to turn the enemy's flank once and for all.' French and English phrases tumbling over each in fiery eloquence like waves being driven to the shore by a storm, he implored the unwinking, stony-faced Frenchman to fight in Paris – it would involve whole German armies – and thus take pressure off the line now held by the British Army.

Reynaud dismissed the suggestion with a wave of his cigarette and behind him the ancient War Minister Marshal Petain, who would soon deliver France to the enemy, growled angrily, 'It would mean the destruction of the country.'

Churchill's flush deepened. The defeatism of the French angered him beyond measure. He had only been in office a month and now the whole alliance with the French was falling apart before his eyes. He wagged a plump finger at Reynaud. 'I will tell you this, Prime Minister,' he growled, 'England will fight on whatever France does. She will never give in — *never*! Our Empire and our fleet are intact. We will continue the struggle for years if necessary until Hitlerism is destroyed.' He shrugged. 'It is possible that the Nazis may dominate Europe, I don't know. But it will be a Europe in revolt, and in the end, it is certain that a regime whose victories are in the main due to its machines and not its men will collapse. Machines will one day beat machines . . .'

As he spoke, Churchill had a sudden vision of utter ruin, dust-clouds over burning, collapsing English cities; but in the far distance he could just glimpse the sun of victory rising over a silent world of dead towns and smoking rubble.

The bulldog Englishman's eloquence had no effect on his French listeners. Reynaud stared woodenly at the centre of the big polished conference table, eyebrows raised but eyes expressionless. The two ancient French marshals, Petain and Weygand, looked into the far distance beyond Churchill, as if they could not wait for him to finish his diatribe. In the end, the British Prime Minister did so. Breaking off in mid-word, he shoved his chair back angrily and snapped at his advisers, 'Gentlemen, I think it is purposeless to continue. Let us leave.' And with that he stalked out before the French even attempted to rise. The Alliance was finished, and the fate of St Valery sealed.

TWO

Rommel focused his glasses on the burning port. It was covered by a white pall of smoke, but here and there he could see the deep-red flames of burning oil dumps and petrol refineries. All the same, there were plenty of Tommies about, running out wire, heaving up sandbags to form new strongpoints all along the quay, and preparing to him what looked like ramps into the water. Were they going to attempt a new 'Dunkirk' after all at this late hour, when the *Luftwaffe* dominated the Channel?

The General frowned and lowered his binoculars thoughtfully. At a secret conference of the commanders in France with Hitler a week before, the *Führer* had told him that he had been worried about his, Rommel's, safety during the Ghost Division's bold drive through France. But Rommel knew all the same that the *Führer* was changeable. If the British managed to get away again it could well mean his removal from command. Hadn't the *Führer* told him that it would be easy to find a basis of peace with the English, once their armies had been smashed?

He swung round and faced the waiting soldiers, who stood in the shade of the poplar trees, out of the heat of the burning sun. 'Major Kranz, Sergeant-Major,' he barked. 'The combination of the 88 and the Mark IV has proved itself these last few weeks. Indeed I am going to suggest to the Inspector-General of the armoured forces that it should be adopted as a standard grouping in the Panzer division. You gentlemen have accidentally hit upon a new form of mobile tactics.'

Von Fromm beamed, but the NCO and Kranz showed no emotion. Their 'new form of mobile tactics' meant little to them.

'Now,' Rommel continued, 'I am going to try out your combination in a very exposed position. It will be dangerous, but I think it will pay excellent dividends. You can see that the Tommies are preparing to defend the port. Presumably they will attempt to evacuate their men from it. That must not happen. Is that clear?'

'Clear,' the three of them answered, wondering what exactly the hard-faced General had in store for them.

'You can also see that they are massing their infantry to cover this height. As the Tommy commander has correctly guessed, it is from here that we will launch our attack on St Valery. Good, I shall give him what he expects — an artillery bombardment followed by the standard infantry attack on his positions.' Suddenly Rommel's foxlike face smiled at his own cunning. 'But with one difference. While the two infantry forces are engaged with each other, an armoured task force, complete with a battery of 88s, will break through the infantry, head by the quickest route for the docks and capture that quay near the burning freighter you can see. That new task force will be yours, Major Kranz. No one has ever tried anything like this before in the history of armoured warfare — a mixed tank-gun force, breaking out ahead of the infantry and doing a job which is traditionally that of the foot-slogger. It will catch the Tommies completely off guard. Now gentlemen, what questions have you?'

Kranz had many questions to ask. Why should the Ghost Division's infantry be sacrificed in a frontal attack? How could a tank-gun force hold out in a built-up area, ideally suited for house-to-house fighting, when it had no covering infantry? But he did not pose them. General Rommel's mind was made up; the stocky Swabian did not take advice from subordinates.

So it was left to an excited von Fromm to ask, his eyes sparkling with barely repressed excitement, 'When do we start, General?'

'In one hour, Captain. I have already made my dispositions. I shall lead the infantry attack myself.'

The red signal flare hissed into the burning June sky. An instant later the whole of the Ghost Division's artillery, positioned on the high ground, crashed into action. The heavy, oppressive afternoon calm was ripped apart savagely. Salvo after salvo rose in hoarse, elemental fury.

The Tommy line disappeared in a cloud of brown smoke. Rommel hesitated no longer. He raised the whistle to his lips and blew shrilly. The whistles sounded all along the long-line of concealed infantry. NCOs and officers rose to their feet, yelling orders. The sweating infantry gripped their rifles more tightly and followed suit. The attack had begun.

Someone cheered. The whole grey line of running men took up the cheer. Somewhere from out of the smoke a slow English machine gun started to chatter. A soldier went down, his hands fanning the air, as if he wanted to wave Death away. Another soldier sat down abruptly, his nickel spectacles slipping absurdly to the side of his suddenly bloody head. Now the cry 'Stretcher-bearer! Stretcher-bearer, at the double!' began to be yelled everywhere, as the English fire rose in intensity.

They ran on, gasping for breath now, springing across the smoking shell holes, knowing that once they were within a hundred metres of the Tommy line, the covering barrage would cease. The chance of hitting their own troops would be too great.

A burst of Vickers fire from the smoke caught the leading company commander in the stomach. He screamed with pain and fell to his knees, yelping with agony. Next instant the phosphorous grenade thrust into his belt exploded. In a flash he was burning like a torch, wreathed in a burning white light. Rommel sprang past the writhing, blazing officer and, pausing momentarily, fired five quick shots from his automatic into the smoke. He knew he would not hit anyone, but he knew too he must encourage the infantry who were staggering past their unfortunate officer now lying consumed in that terrible heat. 'Come on!' he bellowed in an ecstasy of suspense. 'Remember you are the Ghost Division. Follow me!'

Suddenly the barrage from the heights stopped. The running men entered the smoke. Before them the whole Tommy line loomed up out of the rolling brown clouds. Everywhere the Tommies were popping up out of their holes, pushing back their pudding-basin helmets, sighting along their rifle barrels.

Tracer zipped towards the advancing Germans like flights of angry, blood-red hornets. Soldiers skidded to a stop everywhere. Next to Rommel an officer screamed and came to a halt, swaying dangerously. Rommel grabbed him. 'Hold on,' he gasped, 'it's—' He stopped short. The man was dead on his feet, a neat

147

hole drilled through his forehead. Rommel let him fall. Almost gently, he closed the man's eyes and ran on. Now they were almost in the Tommy positions. Overcome by a tremendous, all-consuming rage at the terrible casualties they were taking, the infantry flung themselves at the Tommies, who were now springing out of their pits to meet them.

Bayonet clashed with bayonet. A dwarf of a soldier with the bandy legs of years of poor diet in some Scottish slum or other raced at Rommel, froth foaming at his lips. He screamed a terrible oath and lunged at the General. Rommel side-stepped at the very last moment. He heard the long blade rip along his belt. Next instant he pressed his trigger. The Scot's features disappeared in a mess of gore.

Even at that moment of frightening tension, Rommel remembered again why they had called the Scots the 'ladies from hell' in the old war. There was nothing like the fury of those men when their blood was aroused.

He parried another bayonet, stuck out his foot and, as the soldier stumbled to his knees, blasted the back of his skull off with a neat shot to the right ear.

Now the whole line of field-grey and khaki swayed back and forth, locked in elemental, furious conflict, screaming and snarling at each other in panic-stricken rage. But slowly the Scottish fury was beginning to win the day. The dour Thuringians began to weaken. Rommel, his face lathered with sweat, a powder burn running down the side of his left cheek, his tunic ripped by a bayonet slash, firing to left and right, could 'feel' his infantry start to weaken. He staggered back a few paces with them, yelling, 'Stand fast the 7th! Do you hear me? Stand fast damn you!'

But now the Scots were pressing home their attack with reckless, savage daring. Bayonets flashed in the sun, their blades tipped blood-red. Thuringians went down screaming, writhing as those terrible blades dug deep into their guts. A sergeant ran by Rommel, helmetless and without a weapon, his eyes wild with panic. Rommel grabbed at him — and missed. The sergeant began to scream. 'Run for it, boys . . . run for it, before they slaughter us!'

Rommel screamed an obscenity and fired at the running man's back. Again he missed and the man kept on running and screaming.

It was too much for the Thuringians. They broke everywhere. They had had enough. In a flash, they were streaming back the way they had come, grappling and shoving each other in their haste to get away from that terrible Scottish fury. Reluctantly, Rommel and a few of the older officers covered their flight, firing, withdrawing, firing, withdrawing, until finally the artillery commander on the heights came to their aid. Smoke shells started to explode between them and the Scots, covering the survivors' withdrawal.

But even as he ran after the others, Rommel knew his plan had worked so far. Now it was up to Kranz. He smiled bleakly as he sprang over yet another crumpled body in field-grey, which had been sacrificed to his overweening ambition.

Kranz raised his voice above the roar of the guns, 'Driver,' he commanded, '*advance!*'

To his right and left, the other Mark IVs burst from their camouflaged positions, machine guns already spitting fire. Behind them in the centre of the armoured box, formed by the tanks to front and flanks, Sergeant-Major Schott's towing vehicles lumbered forward, a machine gunner lying precariously on each cab, firing his spandau to left and right in support of the tanks.

The armoured box rolled over the field-greys' dead, churning their bodies to bloody pulp, and on into the thick white smoke. Tommies appeared from nowhere. Here and there little groups of them tried to stand up to the metal monsters. The machine gunners mowed them down and the tracks flailed out their bloody limbs and broken bodies to both sides. The Tommies began to run, flinging themselves into their slit trenches, cowering there, hands pressed tightly about their heads like children trying to blot out some night-time horror.

They burst through the trench line. Ahead, the port loomed up. A burst of tracer caught the gunner on the roof of Schott's truck. He screamed and smashed onto the bonnet like a sack of cement. Schott leaned out, ignoring the slugs pelting against the truck from all sides, and tried to drag him into the cab. But the driver bumped suddenly over some obstacles and the man slipped from sight. Schott bit his lip, but he said nothing. There would be many more dead and abandoned like him before this crazy business was over, he told himself.

The box rolled on.

The tanks rattled down the maze of cobbled back-streets, taking fire from all sides. Grenades bounced off the buttoned-down turrets, exploding harmlessly on the sides. Twice, crazed or courageous Tommies rushed them and tried to climb up the glacis plates of the Mark IVs in order to prise open the hatches; and twice the machine gunners swatted them off with vicious bursts, as if they were flies.

Kranz rapped out order after order over the radio, trying to keep control of his strike force in the confusion of the streets, knowing without being told that Sergeant-Major Schott in his unarmoured vehicles must by now have been taking serious casualties. Undoubtedly all the machine gunners on the cabs — easy targets for the Tommies in the upper storeys on both sides — must be dead or wounded. Now all it needed was one lucky shot on the part of the Tommies and the whole column would be stalled. Then the enemy would have them at their mercy.

The Mark IV swung round a corner. To their front a shabby tin-roof warehouse loomed up. Kranz spotted the Tommy running towards the line of blue-painted cans which barred the road, a signal pistol in his hand. For a moment he could not make out what the man was going to do. Then he understood. 'Knock the bastard out!' he yelled urgently. The gunner fired a quick burst. The Tommy went down, pistol still held in his hand. Groggily he raised his hand. 'Take him out — for God's sake!' Kranz bellowed.

The gunner fired another burst in the same instant that the dying Tommy fired his Very pistol. The cans of paint went up in flames with a great whoosh. In a flash, the whole street was ablaze. And they were trapped.

THREE

The Major held his hand to his bleeding knee, as he made his
excited report. The line had held, except in one place, where
German tanks and guns had broken through. But now the
German advance had run into trouble. The enemy was boxed in
in a side-street just behind the quay.

General Fortune held his peace as he knew a good commander
should, and let the wounded infantryman finish his report. He
had a hundred urgent questions to ask, but one had to be
considerate to subordinates.

He thrust the half-empty bottle of whisky at the Major; it
was his last, but the other man needed it more than he did.
'Here, drink,' he commanded.

The Major took a deep draught and the colour flooded his
grey, pain-racked face once more. 'Thank you, sir,' he gasped
and put the bottle down.

'Now,' Fortune said briskly. 'Where are they located, exactly?
Show me on the map.'

The Major placed a forefinger, tipped with his own blood, on
the map.

'There, sir.'

Fortune stared at the coordinates. It was obvious what the
Germans were about to try. They were moving in to cut him off
from the docks, and he knew that must not happen. He had to
hold out the belief to his hard-pressed Jocks that there might
still be a chance of being evacuated. They would fight harder
with that hope in their hearts.

'One of my chaps, a subaltern named Drummond, managed
to set a paint warehouse on fire just in front of them. He bought
it, poor chap, but now they can't move forward, and bunched
like they are there's not much hope of them moving backwards
either. I've got a couple of Brens and a Vickers in position at the
other end of the street.'

'Very good. But three machine guns won't stop tanks, Major,' Fortune snapped. 'Unfortunately we haven't got any anti-tank guns. We'll have to make do with Molotov cocktails, or something like that.'

'Sir.'

Fortune spun round. It was Farquharson, whose company had been slaughtered the other day at Fécamp and who was now without a command. 'What is it, Captain?' he demanded urgently.

'My guess is, sir, that the Boche will try to break their way out, perhaps through the houses on either side of the street. I know *I* would if I were in their shoes.'

'Yes, yes, get on with it,' Fortune said impatiently.

'Well, sir, we've got no time to make Molotov cocktails, and besides, there's a quicker method of burning them out.'

'How?'

'I know the street well, sir. There used to be a little establishment there—' Farquharson's handsome, young Scots face flushed at the memory and he caught himself just in time. 'Well, sir, there's a French – er – petrol station at one end. I suppose it was used by them to fill up—'

'*Please*, Farquharson,' Fortune cut in brutally.

'Well, sir, if you give me a platoon of infantry, I'll make that petrol station into a flame-thrower for you.' He grinned suddenly, full of youthful high spirits at the prospect of fresh action to avenge the slaughter at Fécamp. 'I'll toast those Boche's balls off them!'

General Fortune grasped at straws. 'You've got my personal headquarters platoon, Captain Farquharson,' he barked.

'Thank you, sir.' The young Black Watch officer grabbed his helmet, put it on, saluted hurriedly and doubled off, not even waiting for the ever courteous General to return the salute. Fortune stared after him and whispered to no one in particular, 'God, please let him pull it off!'

The staff officers stared at each other, eyes full of shock. The General was obviously at the end of his tether.

*

Vicious purple tongues of flame were leaping up everywhere from the shattered buildings. Machine guns chattered. Tracer zig-zagged back and forth crazily, whining off the brick walls. Everywhere there were bodies, German and English, sprawled out in the gutters in the violent abandon of death.

The two running men clattered into a side street. A group of horses, broken out of some stable or other, raced towards them, manes ablaze, eyes bulging out of their heads in panic.

'My God,' von Fromm gasped, as Schott thrust him against the wall and allowed them to gallop by. 'The poor beasts!'

'Forget them,' Schott said grimly. 'Think of our poor lads trapped up there.'

They ran on, eyes searching the street on both sides for some way out, but there was none. On both sides the warehouses and port establishments were protected, presumably against thieves, by high brick walls, topped by broken bottles set in concrete.

Schott skidded to a stop just as the first burst of m.g. fire stitched a blue-sparked pattern across the cobbles to their immediate front. 'Tommy m.g. nest! Up in that second floor window — there!' With a grunt he flung his last grenade. The stick bomb whizzed through the opening. A muffled crash followed, and the Tommy gunner was blown out of the room to smash to the cobbles below.

'Neat,' von Fromm breathed his admiration, 'very neat!'

'But it still doesn't get us out of this mess,' Schott snapped, angry at von Fromm, the Tommies, the whole war for having got him into this bloody situation. He knew he could break out by himself, but his boys and the remaining old men of the original battery did not have a chance in hell of doing so. He would have to do it for them. 'Come on.'

Von Fromm grabbed his arm and held him back. 'My God! Look at that!'

Schott ignored the fire of yet another concealed Tommy m.g. and followed the direction of von Fromm's outstretched hand. To their right, there was a petrol station, already swarming with Tommies, with, at its side, again protected by a brick wall, what looked like a parking lot that ran out onto the quay

153

beyond. Schott could just see the sea through a shell hole in the wall. 'Do you think—'

'Of course,' von Fromm said confidently. 'The Mark IV weighs 20 tons. In bottom gear, it could smash through that wall. After that it's plain sailing. We'd be right on our objective.'

'Then what are we waiting here for like spare pricks in a convent?' Schott bellowed. 'Come on, let's get back to the CO.'

With machine-gun bullets exploding in angry spurts around their heels, the two of them ran back the way they had come, watched by a smiling Farquharson. It looked as if the Boche were going to walk straight into his little trap.

The lone Mark IV swung round the corner, spitting fire. The Tommies fell everywhere as its bullets cythed the street before it. The motor-cycle combination, with Schott in the side-car, had been used to clear a passage for the Mark IV through the mess of trapped vehicles and now shot forward again into the lead. A Tommy in an upper floor leaned out over the street and dropped his grenade neatly in front of it. The driver was catapulted from his seat by the blast and smashed into a gas lamp. There was the hiss of escaping gas, as Schott dived from the wrecked vehicle, rolled out of danger and fired a burst from his m.p. The Tommy in the upper window screamed and slumped down over the sill.

The Mark IV rumbled to a stop. Schott picked himself up. His right leg hurt like hell. He began to limp as quickly as he could towards the waiting tank, the slugs already howling off its thick armour. 'Hurry, man!' the tank commander called from within the tank, '*hurry!*'

There was a strange rattle. Schott paused and looked up the street. A large drum was rolling down the slight incline, straight for the stationary tank. Behind it, some ten metres off, a Tommy was standing with a sub-machine gun held to his right hip like the gangsters Schott remembered from his cinema-going days.

For a moment Schott stood there, puzzled at the reason. The drum rolled ever nearer to the Mark IV. Then the stink of spilled fuel filled his nostrils and he knew what the Tommies were attempting to do. 'Get moving . . . move off without me,' he began. '*Move!*'

The can struck the front of the tank with a hollow clang. Schott raised his m.p. to fire. The Tommy was quicker. He fired from the hip. Red tracer smashed into the drum. The fuel flooded out, spurting up and drenching the glacis plate, filling the air with its choking stench.

For a moment, nothing seemed to happen. Abruptly there was a great gasp, like some huge, primeval monster drawing breath. Next instant the whole tank was ablaze and the tank commander was writhing in agony, trapped in the turret, trying to beat out the flames which wreathed him with hands that were themselves ablaze.

The first attempt to break out had failed.

Kranz looked down at the helmetless, limping Schott and knew immediately that they had failed. 'No?' He mouthed the word carefully.

Schott, his face black with smoke, his eyebrows gone, shook his head miserably.

Kranz looked at von Fromm and then back to Schott. 'What happened?' Swiftly Schott told him about the Tommy-held petrol station and the improvised flame thrower, which had set the Mark IV on fire.

'Heaven, arse and cloudburst!' Kranz cursed when he was finished. 'Why did I ever let the General send us on this mission without infantry!'

'We could tackle them with one of Schott's 88s,' von Fromm suggested.

'Impossible,' Kranz snapped angrily. 'They'd pick off every man in the gun crew from those windows before we had fired out first damn shell!'

'But what?' von Fromm stopped short. There had been a strange soft plop, like a cork being pulled out of a gigantic bottle, to their rear. He looked around, puzzled. Then he spotted it. A small dark object hurtling out of the burning sky. 'Mortar!' he cried, in sudden alarm.

The first salvo came raining down, landing all around the stalled trucks and tanks. In the narrow confines of the street, great angry shards of steel hissed from wall to wall, cutting down everything in their path. Kranz ducked behind the cover of the turret, knowing as he did so that if they did not get out of the street soon, they would simply be slaughtered.

Confident now that he had mastered the situation, Captain Farquharson prepared for the next German breakout attempt, his young face radiating success and pleasure in the ruddy glow of the burning tank. Swiftly he deployed his HQ platoon, all good solid 'terriers' from the north. They were not much good in the attack, but he knew they would fight like the devil himself on the defensive. While the handful of Black Watch from his own company prepared more cans of petrol for the enemy tracks, spraying the pumps the length of the street so that the cobbles were awash with fuel, he positioned his terriers in the houses on both sides of the filling station.

Finally he was satisfied. Raising his voice above the racket the mortar barrage was making, he cried: 'Now, lads, we've got them properly bottled up. This time they'll come on foot, trying to break out that way with the tanks bringing up the rear. But we'll be waiting for them, won't we, lads?'

'Ay, that we will, sir!' the men roared back.

'Good for you,' Farquharson said, highly delighted with himself. He swung round to the waiting piper. 'All right, Brennan,' he commanded the leathery-faced pipe-major, whose skin was baked a permanent brown by a life-time of service in the East, 'gie's a tune, Pipe-Major.'

The bandy-legged musician pumped up his chest like a pigeon preening itself and blew hard into the pipes. As Kranz finally made up his mind about how he was going to try to get out of the trap, his ears were assailed by the strange, unnerving, primitive music of *Highland Laddie*.

FOUR

'In the name of the devil,' von Fromm cursed, 'I don't know which is worse, those mortars or that racket made by the bagpipes. What savages the Scots must be!'

Kranz ignored the comment. Time was running out. The mortar barrage was getting more severe by the minute and his men were huddled everywhere, trying to escape those hellish fist-sized fragments of lacerating steel. 'All right, von Fromm, you know your orders. As soon as you see the signal, you bring up the tanks at once. Clear?'

'Clear. I'd go to hell and back to stop that bagpipe racket.' Kranz turned to the waiting Sergeant-Major Schott. 'All right, Sergeant-Major, take it.'

Schott doubled to the 88, already trained and laid. 'Hands over your ears, gentlemen,' he commanded, 'or you'll be minus a set of eardrums in a minute.' Hardly waiting for them to comply, knowing that anxious, sweating gun-crew was fully exposed to the mortar barrage, he cried, 'Fire!'

The flak gun crashed into action, the great roar it made resounding through the stone chasm. Kranz closed his eyes instinctively, as the hot blast swamped him, his nostrils filled suddenly with acrid fumes. He coughed and opened them again. At that range, the 88 had done exactly what they had planned it should do – blown a huge hole into the high brick wall that fenced them in, and a lesser one in the house behind it.

'Good work,' he shouted. 'All right, you men – follow me.' Kranz doubled forward, followed by the half dozen picked men, each one of them armed with a machine pistol. Clambering over the smoking rubble of the wall, they darted into the house itself and clattered up the stairs. Running through room after room, they reached the top floor.

Panting wildly, Kranz surveyed the ceiling above him, looking for the trap. He had it. 'Pyramid!' he rasped.

Obediently, two of his men bent their backs. He swung himself on them and balancing there, feet astride, Kranz reached up and prised the trapdoor open. A second later he had heaved himself inside the dark loft, which stank of bird droppings and ancient decay, trying to ascertain if anything else but the usual thin brick wall barred any further progress.

He was lucky. An old wall, its mortar badly crumbling, was the only barrier. 'Come on,' he ordered. 'We're in luck. Let's get on with it.'

'Engines!' someone said sharply.

'All right, Pipe-Major, that's enough — thank you,' Captain Farquharson snapped swiftly.

The Pipe-Major took the chanter out of his wet lips and, like the rest, cocked his head to one side to listen intently. Farquharson nodded, his face suddenly gleeful. 'They're coming! It's tank motors all right. Stand by. You, Joad, give the street another drink of petrol.'

'Yessir!' At the pump, the grinning Black Watch private started pumping the lever up and down for all his worth, spraying the street to their front with fresh petrol. 'Best grade juice — one shilling and threepence a gallon, you know, sir.'

In an instant there was the nauseating stench of petrol everywhere, making the men crouched all around the filling station retch drily, as their gaze fixed on the only way that the Germans could come.

The first two houses had been easy. A couple of hefty kicks and the bricks had crumbled, leaving holes big enough for them to crawl through. The wall between the second and third house had been newly cemented up. The way ahead had been barred.

For a moment, Kranz despaired. Then he remembered the roof. Together with his men, he removed a couple of square metres of slate tiles, forcing them loose from the retaining nails until the gap was big enough for them to proceed.

'Socks off and wrap them around your boots,' he ordered. Together, the men whipped off the foot-rags which they wore in the place of

158

socks, replaced their dice-beakers, and swiftly wrapped the bindings around them. 'All right, follow me,' Kranz commanded.

He heaved himself up and onto the warmth of the slate tiles. Gingerly he edged his way along the steep roof until he had reached the security of the chimney. He chanced a glance around it. Down below he could see the enemy positions, clearly outlined against the darkness of the street. He held his finger to his lips in warning and indicated that the others should crawl up to him. They did so. 'All right,' he whispered, 'we'll make it to the roof of the next house. Then we'll be right above the petrol station itself. That's the danger spot. Knock that out and the way's free for the tanks. But for God's sake, watch your step. These tiles are devilishly slippery at this angle.'

The men gulped, faces suddenly pale. One slip, they knew, and they could go sailing over the side of the steep roof to crash down on the cruel cobbles some thirty metres below.

Kranz took a deep breath, trying to avoid looking down at the edge of the roof and the sickening drop beyond, and began to crawl forward, body tilted at a forty-five degree angle against the slope of the roof.

Time passed leadenly. Kranz longed for a moment's pause. The terror of loosing his grip on the slate had brought him out in a lather of sweat. The strain of trying to stay in place without making any noise was tremendous. It seemed as if his objective — the edge of the roof — was as far away as the moon.

Once, he slipped. For one long, agonized moment he thought he could not hold himself. While his men watched, mesmerized, Kranz slithered slowly and apparently inevitably towards the edge of the roof, eyes wild with fear, teeth biting deep into his bottom lip to hold back the shrill cry of fear. Suddenly he stopped. For a second he could not make out what had happened. Then the cold dig of steel into his back enlightened him. His belt had caught in one of the fire hooks welded into the roof so that ladders could be attached in case of emergency. He breathed out a hard-felt sigh of relief following that terrible moment of overwhelming fear.

Steeling himself to make the effort, his heart beating wildly, his eyes blinded with hot stinging sweat, Major Kranz started the long crawl back to the others.

And then they had done it. Chest heaving with the effort, they lay full-length above the petrol station, every detail of the Tommy positions startlingly clear. They were so close that they felt they could reach out and touch them.

Cautiously, Kranz felt for his pistol. 'Prepare to throw the grenades,' he whispered. 'You, Marx,' he looked at the youth to his right, 'take out that Tommy with the sub-machine gun. He's the one who ignites the petrol. And for Chrissake, don't miss the filling station. I don't want that street down there set alight by our own grenades.'

The men were poised with bundles of stick grenades, eyes fixed intently on Kranz's face, as he raised the signal pistol and began to count. '*One . . . two . . .*'

Von Fromm saw the red and green flares burst above the houses and sprang into action. He pressed his throat-mike and began, 'Driver, now get behind it—'

But the driver was already guiding the abandoned French truck forward, bumping it towards the incline down which it would run of its own volition. Creaking and groaning, as if reluctant to move towards the inferno which awaited it, the truck started to gather speed.

Satisfied, von Fromm, standing upright in the turret of the lead tank, oblivious to the shrapnel flying everywhere, pumped his right hand up and down three times, the signal for the column to move off.

'Start up!' Sergeant-Major Schott cried above the noise of the tank engines, 'and driver, for God's sake, keep right behind that tank. That armour *must* protect us. Because this one is going to be really very hairy.'

The attack-force was on its way.

'*Now!*'

Kranz's command rang out above the snap-and-crackle of the skirmish below. As one, the six men raised themselves and flung

160

their bundles of grenades, while Marx took careful aim, as if he were back on some peace-time range, unflustered by the urgency and nervousness of battle.

The grenades exploded in sudden fury all along the Tommy positions. At that range the Germans could not miss. Great gaping holes appeared in their lines everywhere, in the same moment as the abandoned truck started to rattle crazily down the incline, straight for the filling station.

'Knock it out!' Farquharson yelled desperately.

The sergeant with the Tommy gun brought it to the aim. Marx squeezed off a burst. The sergeant went down as if pole-axed, his finger still clutching hard on the trigger so that tracer zig-zagged harmlessly straight into the burning sky. A moment later the truck had crashed full-tilt into the pumps with a sound of rending metal and splintering glass.

'Here they come!' Kranz yelled excitedly. 'Down we go!'

The first tank had appeared round the bend, its machine gun already blazing scarlet flame. While the bombers fled back to the hole they had made, von Fromm drove straight at the filling station. Farquharson pulled out his pistol. The German tank was splashing petrol up on both sides of its track in a stinking red wake. Desperately he took aim, trying to calm his hectic breathing. The tank filled his sight. It blotted out all else, turning day into night. He knew he must drop his pistol and run, if he wanted to survive. But he could not. The tank was only yards away. In the narrow confines of the back-alley, the noise was ear-slitting. Farquharson's every instinct told him to make a run for it. All around, his men were falling back, faces distorted with terror. Yet he knew he must stand his ground. One lucky shot and the whole street would be ablaze — and the German threat to the docks would be stopped. Now the tank was only ten yards away, its machine gun slugs striking the ground all around him. But he seemed to bear a charmed life. They missed him by a hair's breath. He could feel them tugging at his battledress. The tank was almost on him now. The gleam of its cruel rotating tracks blinded him. One second more and he would be churned up under them.

Screaming with fear but with no noise coming from his gaping

161

lips, the young Captain pressed his trigger. Click! The revolver had not fired. In that last flash before he disappeared under the tracks, mangled to a lifeless pulp, he realized he had forgotten to take off the safety catch.

The Mark IV smashed into the side of the filling station and spun round, machine gun chattering. Von Fromm caught himself just in time. 'Advance — driver,' he yelled above the tremendous racket. 'Hit that wall with all you've got!'

The driver needed no urging. Crouched over his controls, ignoring the terror-stricken Tommies fleeing on both sides and the bullets which whined off the glacis plate, he charged the nearest brick wall. The Mark IV hit it with an earth-shaking crash. Von Fromm was flung against the front of the turret. He felt his mouth flood with the salty taste of fresh blood. He shook his head in a daze. The impact had stalled the motor. Almost at once the driver pressed the starter button. Above his head, von Fromm could hear heavy boots clambering up the deck of the stalled Mark IV. A metal object began to hammer on the turret hatch. Fear gripped him and he broke into a cold sweat. In a moment, they would be dropping grenades into the hatch — and that would be the end. 'In the devil's name, driver,' he cried in absolute panic, *start the bastard!*'

Desperately the driver kept punching the starter button, his whole skinny body trembling with fear. Above, a thin blade had been inserted into the turret. Von Fromm watched it, horrified, as if it had a life of its own, as it searched for the spring catch.

Below, the engine coughed.

The tip of the blade had almost found the catch. But von Fromm was paralysed. He could not move. One moment more and the grenades would come tumbling in.

The engine roared into frenetic life. The driver slipped in the clutch. The Mark IV lurched forward. From above, the sudden screams were muffled by the clout of the wall about their heads as the tank surged forward, swatting the Tommies off the brick-littered deck. Another bumb. An angry growl of the racing engine and they were through, veering crazily for the docks ahead, with the rest of the column, guns blazing to both sides, following. Von Fromm mopped the sweat off his brow and grinned.

FIVE

Grimly businesslike, General Fortune handed the German emissary the note. 'Take it,' he said, 'and thank you for coming.'

'But sir, you haven't read it,' the German emissary protested. Outside the guns on the heights opened up again, as if to warn the surrounded Divisional Commander what would be his fate if he did not accept the German terms.

'I don't need to,' Fortune said, politely but firmly. 'Just like the German Army, it is the British Army's duty to fight to the end. You may go now.'

The German shrugged slightly. Tucking the surrender note from Rommel back in his cuff, he saluted and went out to where the staff car, bearing the white flag and surrounded by a group of suspicious Jocks, was waiting to bear him back to the German lines.

General Fortune waited until the man was out of earshot and then made his announcement. 'Gentlemen, the Navy is going to try to take us off tonight.'

'Thank God,' came the murmur. 'The Navy's here.'

'Not quite, gentlemen,' Fortune said carefully, not wanting to dampen their hopes but still not wanting them to believe they were already saved. 'They've got to get into the harbour first.' He turned to his senior brigadier. 'Bill, what is the situation on the perimeter?'

'Not rosy, but we're holding. The cemetery position is doing very well. No trouble whatsoever and we're organizing the odds-and-sods under senior NCOs and putting them into the line wherever it's crumbling. But I doubt if we can hold them much longer in front of that height. Their gunners can see right down our poor chaps' throats. Casualties are high, very high.'

'I see.' General Fortune absorbed the information for a few moments, while outside the German guns increased the intensity of their barrage. Obviously the emissary had returned with his rejection note. 'Tell me, Bill,' he said at last, 'how much time do you think we've got left?' The senior brigadier pursed his lips and looked at his silver pocket watch. 'I'd say about another twelve hours at the max. If the other chap doesn't launch another surprise attack from the heights we'll survive till morning.'

Fortune gave a tired smile. 'It will be long enough. The Navy won't risk any more ships in daylight. I can understand them — the Boche command the air. But if we can hold the perimeter till night falls, we can move back and embark the chaps under cover of darkness.' He cleared his throat and stared around at the suddenly happy looks on his officers' tired, unshaven faces. 'Of course, there is only one fly in the ointment. Those Boche who have broken through to the quay. That could put a spanner in the works.'

'We could run out jetties away from the quay,' someone suggested.

'Like they did at Dunkirk.'

'No good, I'm afraid,' Fortune turned down the suggestion. 'The Boche guns on the heights would soon deal with them. We need the cover of the quay to embark the men in some sort of safety.' His big jaw tightened aggressively, as he draw on his last reserves of strength to impress his will on this pitifully one-sided battle. 'Gentlemen, I anticipate the arrival of the Navy at twenty hundred hours. By then we must have knocked those Germans off the quay or—' He broke off, leaving the rest of his sentence unsaid. But the staff officers knew all too well what the only alternative was.

The setting sun was beginning to slip into the sea. Apart from the muted rumble of the ever present barrage, an ominous silence reigned over the quay. Kranz bit his lips and surveyed his position once again. He had two tanks at each end of the quay, supported by 88mm guns. Two other guns were hidden in the rubble of a warehouse, next to their wrecked, still smoking trucks, their long sinister barrels facing the land. His own tank and one 88mm still attached to the towing vehicle were kept in reserve to move to any spot along the narrow, 200-

metre front under his command. But in spite of his heavy armour, which included the most powerful gun in the world, he still did not have any infantry to cover the many side-streets and narrow alleys which led off the quay between the shattered warehouses. Once darkness fell, his tanks would be sitting ducks for any bold Tommy armed with a sticky bomb or homemade Molotov cocktail.

Kranz, worried and anxious, as the sun started to slip ever deeper beyond the horizon, made a decision. He pressed the button of the throat mike. 'Now get this, all tank commanders. As soon as it's dark, I want you to loose off a flare at five minute intervals in order to illuminate your immediate area. Engines will be kept running, too, in order that you can move out at once if attacked by enemy infantry. One last thing, tank commanders. Each of you will be in position outside – I repeat – *outside* the turret with pistol or machine pistol at the ready. The gunner and driver can cope without you. It will be your job to beat off attacking Tommy stubble-hoppers. Over and out!' He clipped the mike back on its hook and looked up to see Schott staring down at him thoughtfully, glowing cigarette-end carefully concealed in the cup of his big hand. 'When I was a young lieutenant, Sergeant-Major, doing my military service,' he lectured, 'I would undoubtedly have given you three days' arrest on account of that look on your face. Dumb insolence, we used to call the look.' He grinned suddenly, for he had taken a liking to the big Berlin NCO, who, like himself, was obviously a civilian at heart. 'What's on your mind?'

Schott grinned back at him in the blood-red darkness. 'Insolent I might be, Major, but dumb – *no*.'

'Go on.'

'Well, Major. There's something afoot.' He tapped his big nose. 'My old honker hasn't let me down yet. Neither in Poland, Belgium, nor here. The place is too quiet. The Tommies must be up to something.'

Kranz's grin vanished. Slowly he nodded his head in agreement and shivered suddenly, as if he had just experienced a cold breeze. 'I know what you mean, Sergeant-Major. It's too quiet.'

'Too shitting quiet by far. I mean the Tommies know that they can't hold out much longer. There's only one way out for them if they don't want to surrender.' He jerked his big thumb towards the glistening waters of the Channel. 'Why aren't they trying to beat the shit out of us so that they can get to the boats, when they come?'

'*If* they come,' Kranz corrected him.

'*When*,' Schott persisted. 'Half an hour ago, I had to go down to the beach to get a load off my mind.' He made an obscene noise with his lips to indicate exactly what he had been doing down there, 'and I was damn sure that I could hear ship noises out to sea.'

Kranz stroked his unshaven chin thoughtfully. 'You might have been mistaken, Schott.'

The Sergeant-Major shook his big head doggedly. 'Doubt it, sir. My hearing is perfect.'

'All right, but why here? The ships could be going elsewhere.'

'Where?' Schott asked scornfully. 'This is the only place within fifty kilometres where there are Tommies. This is the place they're heading for, and my guess is that they'll be coming in here after dark.' He cast an apprehensive look at the still glittering expanse of water, as if he half expected the British Grand Fleet to appear at any moment. But the Channel was devoid of life, save for a few lone gulls diving mournfully. 'And I'll tell you something else, sir — for free. Once those Tommy ships make an appearance, those fellers inland'll start coming for us with everything they've got. It's their last chance, and believe you me, sir, they're not going to waste it. It's going to be one hell of an effort.'

'Any suggestions?' Kranz forced himself to be as casual as he could, knowing that Schott's mind was working as urgently as his in an attempt to solve the problem.

'Sacrifice the armour in the first place,' Schott said, new urgency in his voice.

'*What?*' Kranz exploded.

'You heard me, sir. The 75mms are going to be no shitty

166

good against the Tommy infantry in the dark, anywhere. Turf the crews out and use them as infantry to cover the quay.'

'Go on!'

'Then turn the 88s around and let them face the sea. Once the Tommy craft get within the port they'll be sitting ducks for my boys.'

'So, in essence, we of the Armoured Brigade should, in your opinion, act as mere infantry screens for your guns?'

'Exactly.'

'But what would General Rommel say?'

Schott looked at the young Major, all the cunning and wisdom of Berlin's back-streets written across his features. 'Major, the Rommels come and go,' he said carefully, 'but the Kranzes and Schotts of this world have got to survive if there's gonna be any kind of purpose in this crazy universe. Let General Rommel have the glory and the honour. All Mrs Schott's big-hearted son wants is to survive!'

Darkness fell like a shroud.

The night was full of a strange, alarming cacophany. Along the quay, there were noises, possibly the sound of running men. Out at sea, shrouded by mist, there were the faint metallic groan of the foghorns. But all were vague, intangible, save for the steady throb of the eight tank engines, ready for instant action.

The defenders were uneasy. At the guns, lined up and pointing out to sea, the crews peered anxiously into the gloom, eyes trying to penetrate it, half-fearful, half-expectant, as if they feared what they might soon see. Grouped round the tanks, facing inland, their task now solely to protect the gun-crews, the tankers dug into the rubble hardly dared move. The Major had ordered them to keep strict silence, telling them it was their only chance to spring a surprise on the Tommy infantry, which undoubtedly outnumbered them.

Kranz, hidden in a half-destroyed shed not more than twenty metres away from his own command tank, its engine ticking away steadily with all the rest, glanced at the green-glowing dial of his wristwatch, time and time again. Surely the Tommies

167

would attack soon? Time was running out for them, too. Why were they waiting? The strain was intolerable. Let the bastards come!

An hour passed, and another. There was a scuttling and whispering everywhere among the ruined warehouses and shed to their front, or so it seemed to a tense, nervous Major Kranz. The whole quayside was alive with the faint noise, like that of rats going about their loathsome, nefarious business. Kranz licked his parched lips and gripped his machine pistol more tightly in sweating hands. Would they never come?

Kranz tensed abruptly. Less than fifty metres away a dark shape had detached itself from the shadows cast by the warehouse wall. Lightly, on rubber soles, the man started running for the command tank. Kranz caught a glimpse of glass. The running man stopped. He grunted. The bottle hurtled through the air. It struck the tank squarely on the turret. For a second, nothing followed the startling smash of breaking glass. Then, in a flash, the tank was ablaze with the exploding Molotov cocktail and the group of running Tommies were silhouetted a stark black against the vicious purple flames.

For one moment the hidden tankers were too startled to react, as more and more Molotov cocktails hissed through the night towards the stationary tanks. Kranz bellowed a hoarse command. A spandau opened up with a high-pitched chatter. Tracer zipped through the darkness. Tommies went down everywhere, screaming, arms and legs flailing in agony, as more and more of them ran out of the alleys and side-streets, crying like crazy men.

The last battle for the beleaguered port of St Valery had commenced in all its terrible fury.

SIX

Rommel lowered his night glasses and the hectic flashes of tracer down at the quayside vanished.

Slowly, the ancient Field Marshal, standing next to him, smelling even at this distance strongly of cognac, lowered his glasses, too.

Rommel waited impatiently while Field Marshal von Rundstedt buried his skinny face deeper in the thick fur collar of his greatcoat, although he himself was sweating in the heat of the June night.

In the end, his impatience got the better of him. 'Well, Field Marshal, what do you think?' he burst out.

Von Rundstedt looked at him coldly. 'What do I think about what, Rommel?' he asked in his goading patrician manner.

'About a final breakthrough to link up with my people now fighting on that quay down there, sir?'

'Oh, that,' von Rundstedt said, as if he were talking about some incident taking place on a remote planet instead of the bloody battle being fought out less than two kilometres away.

'Yessir,' Rommel blurted out. 'One decisive blow now and the English will crumble.' He brought the fingers of his right hand together fiercely, as if he were physically crushing the Tommies to death with them.

Von Rundstedt stared at him, as if he were seeing him for the very first time. 'So you think so, do you?' He said it mildly enough, but an angry, impatient Rommel noted the icy undertone all the same. 'And you are also thinking that you would be sending down tanks into a night attack without sufficient infantry to cover them? What good are tanks in the darkness when any half-trained boy who is brave enough can put them out of action with a grenade? And if that weren't enough, Rommel, that mass of rubble down there would swallow up your whole division— and more— without any positive result. To attack a built-up area one needs infantry. *Infantry*, do you hear, Rommel?' the old man gasped for breath.

Rommel caught the angry words which were about to burst

169

from his mouth in the nick of time. 'But sir, if the Tommies break through the quay, their Navy could well evacuate them under the cover of darkness, and then they would be gone.'

'So?' von Rundstedt said, a note of cynicism in his ancient voice.

'It would be defeat. A division of Tommies vanished under our very noses. What would the *Führer*—'

'Rommel,' von Rundstedt interrupted him, 'take the advice of an old man who has been a soldier nearly fifty years. Place not your trust in politicians.' With a wave of his grey-gloved hand, he indicated his aide should leave them, so that he could talk more freely. 'Place your trust in your men, your command, the Army. Give them your loyalty and you will receive loyalty in return.' He paused thoughtfully, wondering just how to phrase his next words. 'You are a young man, Rommel,' he continued. 'You thirst for glory and high command, I can see that. And you have great gifts, but do not waste them following false prophets. It might well be the end of you.'

Inwardly Rommel raged with frustration. What right had this ancient alcoholic to lecture him? he asked himself angrily. Had not Rundstedt's aristocratic, traditional military connections always ensured he would be promoted to the highest command, while *he* had had to spend bitter years working his way up the chain of command – ten years from captain to major alone! Now there was the chance of great glory – and promotion – within grasping distance, and the old fool was forbidding him to take it. Never again, he told himself at that moment of supreme disappointment, would he allow anyone else to rein him in just as he was about to pass the winning post first.

His voice icy and constrained, Rommel brought the conversation to a close. 'Your orders, Field Marshal?'

'Attack at dawn.'

Casually he acknowledged Rommel's immaculate salute with a weak touch of his gloved hand to his cap and began to walk back to his waiting car, while Rommel stared straight ahead, fists gripped white-knuckled with rage.

Down below the fight for the quay raged on. There were six more hours till dawn.

*

By now, every last tank was ablaze. In the light of the flickering flames, Kranz could see heaps of dead Tommies sprawled across the cobbles. But still they kept coming, urged on by their angry officers and the weird, blood-curdling wail of the pipes. Attack after attack was stemmed only at the very last moment; and each time the number of Kranz's tankers got fewer and fewer.

A burst of tracer howled off the front sprocket of the wrecked command tank. Blue sparks flew everywhere. Next to it a box of ammunition exploded. Bullets hurtled into the air, ricocheting crazily off the warehouse walls. 'Great flying shit!' von Fromm gasped, his sweat-lathered face coloured a brilliant white in the reflected light. 'They'll be throwing the kitchen sink at us next.'

Behind him, a tanker started to scream. '*My foot . . . my rotten foot has fallen off . . .*'

Kranz gulped. The noise of the casualties was almost unbearable. How much longer could both sides stand this? This wasn't a battle; it was a massacre.

'*Sir!*' a hysterical voice screamed urgently somewhere to his right. '*Armour. They're bringing up tanks.*'

Von Fromm looked at Kranz in utter disbelief. 'But they *can't*!' he cried. 'They haven't *got* tanks, have—'

He stopped short. A squat, open armoured vehicle was rattling out of a side-street, machine gun blazing from a slit next to the driver.

'Bren-gun carrier!' Kranz exclaimed, recognizing the little armoured infantry transporter that the British Army used, in the same moment that half a dozen German machine guns turned on it, slugs howling off its bullet-proof armour in crazy profusion.

A tanker dropped his weapon. For one frightening moment, Kranz thought his men were going to break and flee. But no. The youth doubled forward. Zig-zagging madly like a football player, he avoided the Bren-carrier's machine gun. He sprang up and onto the glacis plate in the same moment that the rattled driver braked hard and hit his face on the wheel. The carrier skidded and smashed into a wall. The tanker screamed hysterically, as he was thrown off onto the cobbles at its side. Next instant, the bayonets of the following infantry flashed in the flickering light. In, and in again.

He screamed piteously, his spine arched in agony, as those cruel blades plunged towards him once more.

Kranz had no time to consider the fate of the unknown tanker, brave as he was. The rattle of tracks was coming from virtually every alley. The Tommies were pushing home a major attack, with more bren-carriers. He did not hesitate. Rising to his feet, ignoring the danger, he shouted his orders. 'Move back . . . nice and slow. Move back everywhere, men!'

It was now four hours till daylight—and what was left of Kranz's command had their backs to the water.

There was no mistaking the sound of ships' engines now. Schott strained his eyes. It seemed to be coming from his right. He could hear it quite clearly, even above the noise of the small arms battle raging to the rear.

'Stand by—all guns!' he bellowed. Elbowing the gun-layer away from behind the telescope, he took the man's place himself. He had no idea what kind of ships were out there. But his guess was that they were armed. If they attempted to anchor in the port, it would be the gunner who got off the first shell that would count.

The steady, pulsating hum came ever closer. Schott had the impression that it was getting slower, too. He pressed his eye even tighter to the telescope, so much so that it hurt. But he did not let up. He had to spot the enemy ship first!

And there it was. A lean shape looming up out of the gloom, a lone light glinting from its forepeak. A Tommy destroyer.

Furiously he swung the long barrel of the 88mm round, crying, 'Now don't let me down, lads. This is it!'

He tensed and jerked the firing bar. The 88mm erupted. Scarlet flame shot out of the muzzle. Yellow smoke flooded the rear of the gun. Schott closed his eyes instinctively. When he opened them again, the destroyer was rocking violently, a huge hole ripped in her rakish bow, flames already beginning to lick along the upper deck. He had scored a direct hit.

His men roared jubilantly, as gun after gun opened up, sending the lone destroyer rolling furiously from side to side, as huge spouts of boiling white water shot into the night air. With a roar like a gigantic express train, a great 16-inch shell hissed over their heads and crashed down far to the rear, dragging the very air out of their lungs as it howled past.

'Jesus, Maria, Joseph!' a terrified Bavarian voice said in the suddenly glowing darkness. 'A battleship— the Tommies have got a battleship out there!'

'Keep on firing!' Schott cried desperately. 'That battleship is not going to attempt to come in any closer. They're firing blind. Knock out the destroyer and the Tommies will take off like a bat out of hell. *Fire!*' Furiously he whirled the wheels round and sighted on the burning ship once more, knowing as he did so that one lucky shot from the enemy guns was all that they would need to reverse the situation.

The 88s fired again. It was now just over three hours to dawn. The battle continued.

General Fortune was desperate. By the hissing white glare of the paraffin lamp he stared at the map of the docks and the thin red arrows which indicated the advance of his infantry. There were only two more hours until dawn, and he knew that once it was light the destroyers which had come to take off the Division would sail out to sea before the German air raids began. Yet his men had still not cleared the quay. He wiped his unshaven chin. 'Rennie,' he said to the anxious major standing next to him, 'what have we got left in the kitty?'

'Nothing,' Rennie answered bluntly.

'But you *must* have, man.'

'I haven't, General. The line's crumbling everywhere along the perimeter and it's obvious Jerry's going to launch an all-out attack at dawn.'

'But we must break through to the sea *before* dawn. We've had it otherwise.' He looked at the other man, pleading. 'I need more manpower down there.'

'But, sir, I've told you— we have no more reserves left, except perhaps—' Rennie stopped short.

Fortune grabbed at straws. 'Except what?'

'The wounded – down in the cellars.' Rennie bit his lip.

'Of course!' Fortune remembered his own days as a young subaltern in this very same division. 'Uncle Harper's boys', they called themselves so gaily then, after the Divisional Commander. How often they had called upon the lightly wounded to go back into the line when a German attack was on. 'Come on,' he cried, 'into the cellars. We've no time to lose. Any man who can hold a rifle is worth his weight in gold at this particular moment.'

The cellar was packed full of wounded men. It was hot, fetid and stank of blood, urine, ether and pain. The men lay sprawled on the stone floor in blood-stained straw, some moaning, some smoking silently, looking straight ahead, some immobile, perhaps dead. To the rear, two harassed doctors, their aprons red with blood, were hacking away at a shattered leg, their saws rasping into the bone, as the orderly held up a lantern to allow them to see. It was the kind of sight Fortune thought would have ended at Trafalgar— but he knew very well that it was part and parcel of any war.

'The General,' Rennie announced.

Here and there a man tried to rise and stand to attention. Urgently, Fortune waved for the men to lie where they were. 'Good morning, chaps,' he said, as courteous as ever.

'Good morning, sir,' the answer came back, loyal and uncomplaining.

Fortune gulped and felt as if he wanted to turn tail and run. Whatever happened in the next two hours, most of the men here would have to be left behind anyway. But he forced himself to make his announcement.

The response was overwhelming. Grievously wounded men, some with great wads of blood-soaked bandages pressed to their stomachs, others with rough splints attached to shattered legs, staggered to their feet and stumbled towards the door where a pile of weapons lay, abandoned by the stretcher-bearers. One by one they picked them up, grimacing with pain as they did so, and vanished into the red gloom.

Fortune could stand it no more. He turned and fled, his eyes filled with burning tears.

SEVEN

An ominous silence prevailed over the small sector of quay still left in German hands. The only sound was the crackle of the flames and the regular stomach-churning thud of the guns.

Major Kranz, his left arm hanging limp at his side, blood dripping steadily from the rough bandage to the ground, could see the enemy fairly clearly now beyond the piles of bodies, German and British. The firing was dying away, but he knew that this was not the end of the attack. He could sense it in the very air; they would come again.

'How are we placed, von Fromm?' he asked his second-in-command.

Von Fromm, his monocle gone, a lank strain of blond hair hanging down his dirty face, answered wearily, 'A dozen left unwounded, sir. One man to every ten metres.'

'Ammo?'

'Perhaps two and a half mags per man — and a handful of grenades still left.'

'Machine-guns?'

'Two left.'

'Ammo?'

The weary litany continued as the first dirty streaks of the false dawn start to flood the sky, and in the enemy positions, the wounded began to hobble into their positions.

Kranz nodded his head in thanks and handed von Fromm the little tin of brown pills that he had saved till now. 'It's all I've got to offer the men,' he said weakly. 'Benzedrine tablets. You'd better take one yourself.'

Von Fromm accepted them numbly and disappeared into the gloom to distribute them to the weary survivors. Major Kranz swallowed his own pill, feeling as though he could have slept, at this moment, for eternity — and realizing full well that that might just soon be his fate.

Unafraid, uncaring, unutterably weary, he stared to his front through red-rimmed eyes, waiting for the attack that must come.

Now Schott was reduced to two guns. All the rest had been damaged or destroyed by the deadly 16-inch shells from the enemy ship. To his front the destroyer was still sinking slowly, her superstructure a tangled, blazing mass, the water all around her full of bobbing heads. But the destroyer's place had been taken by even more dangerous enemies. Swift British torpedo boats came racing out of the fog at 60 knots, bows high in the air, machine-guns spitting death, breaking to one side in a huge white wave at the very last moment. The dead all around Schott bore eloquent testimony to their effectiveness. On his own gun, only the loader and himself were left. The rest of the crew lay sprawled in the extravagant postures of death among heaps of spent shell cases.

'Here they come again, Sergeant-Major!' a voice at the other gun sang out in alarm.

Schott opened his weary eyes.

Three dark shapes, bows high out of the water, cleaving the white foam at a tremendous rate, were hurtling towards them, guns blazing. Instinctively Schott pulled the firing bar. The 88mm thundered – and missed by fifty metres. He ducked as a hail of bullets from the torpedo boats' twin Brownings peppered the metal shield. Next to him the loader screamed and went reeling back, his face riddled to a pulp. Across the way, the two remaining crew members of the other gun were slumped over their breech.

As the three boats swung round, a huge cascade of flying water descended upon the shield of his gun like a sudden rain storm. Schott dropped his hand from the firing bar helplessly. His battery was finished. There was nothing he could do. The 6th Flak Battery existed no more.

'*Scotland for ever!*' the hoarse cry went up on all sides. The lone piper, a blood-stained bandage around his head, pumped up his pipes and launched into a spirited reel.

'*Scotsmen wae hame!*' a little, bow-legged Glaswegian cried in a cracked voice. 'Come on, lads, let's sort yon Jerry bastards out the nu!'

In a great rush, the halt, the lame, and the crazed surged forward. Immediately the two remaining spandaus started chattering. Men went down on all sides. But there seemed no stopping the impetus of that wild charge. Kranz sprang to his feet. It was now or never. Feeling the adrenalin of fear pump through his blood, he fired point-blank into the oncoming mass. Still the screaming Scots came on.

'Back!' he cried above the roar, snapping off single shots to left and right, even in that moment of extreme danger counting the bullets he had left. 'Back – *for God's sake!*' Firing as they went, the handful of survivors retreated towards a large wrecked warehouse, overlooking the water. They streamed inside, the crazed Scots only a dozen metres behind them, kept at bay like a pack of howling dogs by the Germans' sporadic fire.

A Scot grabbed a gunner by the hair where he lay slumped over the 88 and then let his head fall again. 'Dead,' he cried to the men swarming all around the shattered guns.

'Yon's a guid Jerry,' someone exclaimed in a cracked voice. 'Come on!' They ran on.

Now their bullets were chipping slivers of wood everywhere out of the top floor, while the defenders cowered near the smashed windows, bodies tensed against the flying lead. Now and then, Kranz loosed off a single shot at the encroaching Scots. He clipped home his last magazine, with a slow, deliberate movement. He felt unutterably weary. All he longed to do was to sleep. Death would be a blessing.

'Set the bluidy place alight!' a hoarse voice called from outside.

'Ay,' a hundred other voices took up the cry. 'Burn the Jerry buggers out!'

'*No!*' von Fromm screamed in English. Ignoring the lead flying everywhere, he positioned himself in full view at the window and fired a whole magazine at the mob down below before Kranz pulled him to the floor with the last of his strength. 'But they're going to burn us alive!' von Fromm yelled and then broke down, sobbing like a child.

Kranz rubbed his head with a shaking hand. What was he to do? Down below he could hear the Tommies scuttling about, looking for material to stoke the fire. The horror of the prospect broke through his paralysing weariness. He had to do something. He levered himself up, leaving von Fromm to sob on the floor, and staggered to the window. 'Please,' he began in his rusty school English, 'please, do not burn us. We will come and—'

He stopped abruptly. From further inside the port, its houses now clearly outlined against the grey dawn, a strange sound was floating towards him. The Scots heard it, too, and stopped what they were doing. They were looking at each other, the wildness gone from their sweating, dirt-stained faces, as if they could not believe what it was they heard. Slowly they dropped the burning torches from reluctant fingers. They flickered and went out unnoticed on the debris-littered cobbles. Weapons followed. Here and there a soldier leaned his weary head against a bullet-pocked wall and sobbed.

It seemed to take the battle-weary German Major an age to understand what that bugle was sounding, its silver note ringing true and clear in the still dawn air. But when the men who moments ago had been about to burn them alive in their hiding place started to drag wearily back the way they had come, their path littered with abandoned rifles, he understood at last.

The bugler was sounding the cease-fire. St Valery had surrendered, and they were saved.

EIGHT

In awe the survivors stared at that scene of death and destruction, as the crimson sun rose over the horizon and bathed them in its bloody hue, surveying it in a profound silence, broken only by the soft whimpering of a wounded man hidden somewhere in the piles of dead.

There were dead everywhere – German and Scottish. Some corpses, khaki and field-grey mixed inextricably together, lay on their backs as if they were sleeping. Others were at the water's edge, being nudged back and forth gently by the waves. And over it all hung the terrible stench of spilled blood and mutilated flesh. There was no escape from the smell of death, for there was not a breath of air to dissipate it.

Slowly, Sergeant-Major Schott, his forehead covered with clotted blood, stumped towards the handful of tankers standing outside the warehouse, the sound of his boots echoing eerily across the quay.

Formally he drew his big frame up to the position of attention in front of the gaunt Major, empty pistol still clutched in his hand. 'Sergeant-Major Schott reporting, sir,' he said, his voice hollow and toneless. 'The 6th Flak Battery no longer . . . exists.' He swept a hand helplessly in the direction of the line of shattered guns, with the piles of dead scattered all around them.

Kranz touched his pistol to his right temple. 'Thank you, Sergeant-Major,' he said in a voice that was equally hollow and toneless. He waved the pistol. 'Follow me,' he ordered.

Eyes lifeless, faces grey and worn beyond description, the handful of survivors began to trudge like walking ghosts towards the sound of the advancing tanks.

'So far, *Herr General*,' the excited aide exclaimed, reading from his list, 'we have rounded up twelve thousand prisoners, including eight thousand British from the 51st Division. We have taken twelve generals too, four of them divisional commanders, one British and three French, and the French commander of the 9th Army Corps. Our check is only a rough one, but there seem to be about 1133 trucks, most damaged, in our hands, and about a thousand guns, of various calibres.' He paused and beamed at his commander. 'And would you believe, sir, that we've also sunk a Tommy destroyer! I doubt if any other division in the whole of the *Wehrmacht* can make a claim like that. Indeed it is a great victory for the 7th Panzer!'

'It is indeed,' Rommel agreed, taking his eyes off General Fortune and his staff who were facing defeat with typical English *sangfroid*, laughing and joking in front of their HQ. 'The Ghost Division has proved itself to even its most bitter critics. There is absolutely no doubt about that now.'

'Yes, General,' the aide said. 'We have also made a count of—'

Rommel waved the over-eager young officer silent. 'Later,' he murmured. 'Later.'

Slowly and alone, he walked past the lines of gutted transport and the shattered 88s, their barrels flayed like sticks of peeled celery, and stared out across the shimmering sea. Was this *it?*, he asked himself. Or was there something ahead of him out there, across the narrow stretch of water that divided Germany from her last enemy. He was nearly fifty. Would he end his career as a divisional commander, to become a footnote in some obscure history of the Second War. *'General E. Rommel, Commander 7th Pz. Div, 1939–1940'*. Was that all that destiny held for him?

Strangely despondent, in spite of his great victory, he walked slowly to his command car. 'We depart,' he said tonelessly, and got in.

Slumped in the back, seeing nothing, hearing not even the cheers of a group of engineers busily cracking open cases of captured Scottish whisky, he let himself be borne out of St Valery, his mind full of strange forebodings.

'There he goes, the General,' one of the handful of survivors said, as the big Mercedes swept by them in a swirl of grey dust. No one attempted to rise.

Instead they remained slumped at the verge, some of them too weary even to drink the bottles of looted alcohol which were everywhere.

'Undoubtedly it is a great victory,' von Fromm attempted to put a note of enthusiasm in his voice and failed lamentably. 'The Tommies are finished in Europe.'

Next to him, Schott, his lips a startling red against his dust-covered face, put down the bottle of Scotch he was drinking and shook his head. 'I might be half-pissed, Captain,' he pronounced his words carefully in the manner of drunken men, 'but I think you're wrong. The Tommies don't give up so easily.'

'What *do* you mean, Sergeant-Major? We've run them out of the Continent for good,' von Fromm said again.

'No. They'll come back, Captain. Believe you me, they'll come back. This shitting war isn't over by a shitting long chalk . . .'

EPILOGUE

The infantry, burdened down by heavy packs and large, old-fashioned solar topees, staggered up the sand-hill, their strained faces crimson with the effort, their strange khaki uniforms black with sweat. Behind them rolled the tanks, fighting the steep slope, sand spurting up in a blinding wake behind them. General Rommel knew they were German Mark IVs. But their camouflage was unlike anything we had seen in the *Wehrmacht* before, and the usual German insignia was missing. His frown deepened. What was all this about? Sitting next to him in the tiny cinema, General Schmundt, the *Führer*'s ADC, smiled his amusement. He could just imagine what Rommel was thinking at this particular moment, as the secret training film whirred on. Why the devil had he, the victor of St Valery, been invited to come to the War Ministry in Berlin to view this mystery?

The scene changed. A group of half-naked soldiers, their white upper bodies dripping with sweat, were lining up in front of a severe-faced officer, water-bottles held at the ready. In the corner of the film, white-lettering proclaimed suddenly: *'Water ration per man — two litres!'*

As if to emphasize the heat, the cameras zoomed up above the half-naked men's heads to depict what looked like a battery of huge sun-lamps attached to the roof of some gigantic greenhouse.

'But that's a damn glasshouse!' Rommel could not hide his bewilderment any longer. 'They're training in a glasshouse, Schmundt! What the devil is all this?'

'Be patient, my dear Rommel. Patient. All will be clear in one moment,' Schmundt appeased him.

Now the film started to close. There were a few quick shots of the strange, sweating soldiers digging out tanks bogged down in the sand, laying metal tracks, taking meagre showers from perforated ration cans balanced in what looked like dwarf palmtrees, and then there was one long shot of suddenly snowy landscape and a familiar yellow-and-black German road sign: '2 Kilometres to Baltrum'. The screen went blank.

'Good God!' Rommel exclaimed, 'that film was shot on our own Baltic coast!'

Schmundt clicked his fingers for the lights and turned to a very puzzled General, with an amused smiled on his face. 'Exactly, my dear Erwin. That particular burningly hot desert is located no more than one hundred and fifty kilometres from the spot where we are sitting at this very moment.'

Rommel rose to his feet, his fingers toying angrily with his new Knight's Cross, and looked down at the other man. 'Now Schmundt, enough of this foolishness. You haven't dragged me all the way from my post in the depths of winter to play jokes on me. What in the devil's name is going on here? Out with it, man!'

Schmundt held up his well-manicured hands for peace, the grin still on his face, in spite of the look of rage on Rommel's. 'Hold your horses,' he said. 'All will be revealed to you in due course. Now this—'.

He stopped short. The great double doors had been flung open by two helmeted giants in the black uniform of the SS. Another SS man, even taller than the first pair, strode through the door imperiously, and barked at the top of his voice at the two startled generals. *'Der Führer!'*

The two generals snapped to attention as Adolf Hitler and his whole entourage swept in: the gross Air Marshal Goering, Admiral of the Fleet Raeder in his old-fashioned wing-collar, wooden-faced Keitel and his cunning, pale-eyed running mate, Colonel-General Jodl. They were all there, and Rommel knew there was a flap on. Something big *must* be happening. But he had no time to speculate, for Hitler was already getting down to business. 'Has he seen it now?' he rapped at Schmundt.

'Yes, *mein Führer.*'

'Excellent.' Hitler thrust out his hand and took Rommel's. 'It is good to see you again, General. You look well and rested.'

'Thank you, *mein Führer.*'

'And your blood pressure?' Hitler suddenly sprang the

question on the already bewildered officer. 'Is it back under control, Rommel?'

'Why . . . yes, *mein Führer*,' Rommel managed to stutter.

'Excellent,' Hitler said again, and snapped his fingers.

The screen flooded white. A moment later a map of the Mediterranean flashed onto it. 'Be seated, please, gentlemen,' Hitler commanded, allowing the gigantic SS officer who was his bodyguard to slip a chair beneath him. 'Raeder,' he spoke to the Admiral, 'please begin.'

Raeder tugged at his wing-collar and commenced his briefing. 'As most of you gentlemen present know, we have decided to cancel Operation Sea Lion[1], with the Führer's approval.'

Rommel had not known that Hitler no longer intended to invade England but obviously everyone else had. They all seemed to take the announcement in their stride, at least.

'But we must ensure that England sues for peace, and soon,' Raeder continued. 'But where, if we don't intend to invade the Island? In the opinion of the Naval Staff, the best way to strike at her is to exclude her from the Mediterranean. The British have always considered the Mediterranean the pivot of their world empire, and presently it is only in that area that she is showing any desire to fight. Using her old traditional tactics, she is attempting to strangle the weak. In this case our ally, Italy.'

There was a snigger of contempt from some of the high officers present.

Hitler frowned and the sniggers died away as quickly as they had begun.

'As we all know, from the most recent reports, the Italians have suffered a serious defeat here, in Libya. At first they refused our help, now they need it desperately.' Raeder cleared his throat importantly. 'The Mediterranean must be now cleared up. From Gibraltar to the Suez Canal we must take all British positions. And the Italians cannot do it alone.'

Hitler nodded his head excitedly. 'An advance from Suez,' he broke in, 'through Palestine and Syria, as far as Turkey, is

[1] Code-name for the invasion of Britain.

necessary. If we reach that point, Turkey will be in our power. Then the Russian problem will appear in a different light.' He looked significantly at his entourage. Rommel caught the look but was as puzzled as ever, even though it had long before begun to dawn upon him that he had been called to Berlin for more than just to view a strange sort of Army training film.

Raeder continued. 'Our *Führer* has long realized that we must prevent any real Italian defeat in North Africa. When Sidi-Barrani fell last month, we offered Signor Mussolini German anti-tank units. After the fall of Bardia two weeks ago, we promised them more. Now it looks as if we must make an all-out effort to prevent them from being chased out of Africa altogether.' Raeder stopped and looked at Hitler, as if they had agreed in advance that it would be at this particular moment in the briefing that the *Führer* should take over.

Hitler seized his cue. Rising to his feet, even before the giant SS officer had managed to pull back his chair, he stared directly at Rommel with those dark, hypnotic eyes of his. 'General,' he snapped, 'what you have just witnessed is part of the training programme for two entire divisions – the 5th Light Motorized Division and the 15th Panzer Division. For nearly two months now, we have been secretly preparing them for war in the desert.' Hitler smiled suddenly. 'I think, General, you could do with a little sunshine – and serious exercise, too. It would be good for your rheumatism – and, as I hinted, your blood pressure.'

Rommel's heart leapt. He could hardly believe the sudden welter of possibilities that raced through his mind. 'What exactly do you mean, *mein Führer?*' he gulped.

'I mean, my dear Rommel, how would you like to go to Africa, to North Africa, to be exact, and pull Italy's chestnuts out of the fire for them?' Hitler's dark eyes bored into his face, as if he were issuing his General with a formal challenge, a personal duel of wits and resilience.

'With what, sir?'

'With those two divisions I have just told you about, joined together to form a new corps.'

188

'I accept, of course!' Rommel said without hesitation, knowing that he would never get a chance like this again. A corps of his own! 'And the name of the new corps, *mein Führer?*' he added.

Hitler did not answer at once. He knew the High Command had simply allotted a number to the corps to be formed from the 5th Light and the 15th Panzer. But a number did not appeal to his romantic soul; it was too conventional. This corps would be something special, the first German unit to fight in Africa since 1915. It deserved something more than a mere number. 'It's name, Rommel?' he pondered slowly, his dark face thoughtful. 'I will tell you. It is one that will undoubtedly go down in history . . . It will be . . .'

Rommel waited expectantly, knowing with the clarity of a vision that his hour of destiny had struck.

The German Afrika Korps . . .

All Futura Books are available at your bookshop or newsagent, or can be ordered from the following address:
Futura Books, Cash Sales Department,
P.O. Box 11, Falmouth, Cornwall.

Please send cheque or postal order (no currency), and allow 22p for postage and packing for the first book plus 10p per copy for each additional book ordered up to a maximum charge of 92p in U.K.

Customers in Eire and B.F.P.O. please allow 22p for postage and packing for the first book plus 10p per copy for the next six books, thereafter 4p per book.

Overseas customers please allow 30p for postage and packing for the first book and 10p per copy for each additional book.